Tap, tap, tap...

The sound came from the window. Heart hammering, Harlow stiffened. "What's that?"

Wes grabbed his gun from the table, his expression focused and determined. He handed off his cell. "Call Ranger Kelly and get him out here."

"What are you going to do? What's the plan?"

"I'm going to check the perimeter. You stay here, quiet and hidden." He eyed the gun in her hand and leveled his gaze on her.

"And shoot to kill."

Rocky Mountain K-9 Unit

*These police officers fight for justice
with the help of their brave canine partners.*

Detection Detail by Terri Reed, April 2022
Ready to Protect by Valerie Hansen, May 2022
Hiding in Montana by Laura Scott, June 2022
Undercover Assignment by Dana Mentink, July 2022
Defending from Danger by Jodie Bailey, August 2022
Tracking a Killer by Elizabeth Goddard, September 2022
Explosive Revenge by Maggie K. Black, October 2022
Rescue Mission by Lynette Eason, November 2022
Christmas K-9 Unit Heroes by Lenora Worth and Katy Lee,
December 2022

Elizabeth Goddard is the award-winning author of more than thirty novels and novellas. A 2011 Carol Award winner, she was a double finalist in the 2016 Daphne du Maurier Award for Excellence in Mystery/Suspense and a 2016 Carol Award finalist. Elizabeth graduated with a computer science degree and worked in high-level software sales before retiring to write full-time.

Books by Elizabeth Goddard

Love Inspired Suspense

Rocky Mountain K-9 Unit

Tracking a Killer

Honor Protection Specialists

High-Risk Rescue

Mount Shasta Secrets

Deadly Evidence
Covert Cover-Up
Taken in the Night
High Stakes Escape

Coldwater Bay Intrigue

Thread of Revenge
Stormy Haven
Distress Signal
Running Target

Visit the Author Profile page at LoveInspired.com for more titles.

TRACKING
A KILLER

ELIZABETH
GODDARD

LOVE INSPIRED SUSPENSE

INSPIRATIONAL ROMANCE

Special thanks and acknowledgment are given to Elizabeth Goddard for her contribution to the Rocky Mountain K-9 Unit miniseries.

LOVE INSPIRED® SUSPENSE
INSPIRATIONAL ROMANCE

Recycling programs
for this product may
not exist in your area.

ISBN-13: 978-1-335-58862-3

Tracking a Killer

Love Inspired
22 Adelaide St. West, 41st Floor
Toronto, Ontario M5H 4E3, Canada
www.LoveInspired.com

Printed in U.S.A.

And above all things have fervent charity among yourselves:
for charity shall cover the multitude of sins.
—*1 Peter* 4:8

This book is dedicated to Jesus who died for me while I was still a sinner. He died for us all "while we were yet sinners."

ONE

"I know it's been a long day of travel, girl, but our services are needed." Harlow Zane secured Nell, her beagle specializing in cadaver detection, in the back of her rental Jeep.

Harlow and Nell were part of the Rocky Mountain K-9 Unit mobile team under contract to the FBI. They had assisted on cases within the far-reaching terrain of the Rockies, but this was her first high-profile assignment.

Since early spring, several blondes had been abducted from the Rocky Mountain region's parks. No evidence, no leads. After Emery Rodgers was found strangled in New Mexico, the other women were feared dead, and a task force had been formed to find what might be a serial killer—before he struck again.

But he had. A Grand Teton National Park ranger had recently been abducted. Blonde and blue-eyed, like the previous victims.

Harlow reached out to run her hand through the white-and-tan fur on Nell's neck and around her floppy ears. "We're part of an FBI task force," Harlow said to her partner. "You understand more than some people think, and I know you won't let me down."

This morning, she and Nell had taken a jet from Denver, Colorado, where the RMKU team was based, to Jackson, Wyoming. It was already much later in the afternoon than she would have liked. She glanced at her watch. The sun would be close to setting by the time she arrived at the site in question, so she wouldn't waste another minute getting there. Although cadaver dogs could pick up the scent of human remains that had been in the ground for years, time was of the essence if they wanted to stop a killer in the park.

She shut the back of the Jeep where she'd secured Nell in her crate, gave a little wave to her beagle through the window and then got into the driver's seat. She headed out of the Jackson Hole Airport and north on the state highway toward Yellowstone National Park. According to GPS, she still had a couple of hours before she made it to the plot of ground where Nell's skills would be required. At least by the time she got there, she would still have some daylight.

Being on the RMKU mobile K-9 team meant traveling to locations to search, therefore she should be accustomed to this by now, but Harlow was anxious to get to work so she and Nell could prove themselves. Not that they hadn't already, but being placed on this specialized task force to catch a killer could open more doors. They had to demonstrate that they were more than competent. Harlow needed to exceed expectations—over and over—after that one defining incident in her past. One day she would get beyond it. Maybe this investigation was exactly what she needed to do just that.

Her palms grew slick on the steering wheel as tension built in her shoulders.

Relax...you got this. You and Nell, that is.

She blew out a deep breath and let the stunning scenery calm her nerves. Colorado was beautiful, but she spent a lot of time in the mile-high city of Denver with its skyscrapers, noise and traffic, but the mountains in the distance stood behind a veil of haze.

To her left, Grand Teton—the prominent mountain often depicted in landscape paintings and photographs—stood tall and lofty and close. The sun hit the peak just right, emphasizing the lenticular clouds that sat on the top like a big white cap.

The sight took her breath away.

While the scenery was stunning, she needed to think about this assignment. Though Nell was the only cadaver dog on the RMKU, Harlow still struggled to believe that she and Nell had been selected to help with this case.

She smiled as she drove, recalling the moment Tyson Wilkes, who led the RMKU, had caught her just before she'd left for the day.

He'd been so serious when he'd explained that he'd selected her for this specialized FBI task force to find and stop a killer, and that he had every confidence in her. Tyson never played favorites, but he had a way about him that made everyone feel like they were special. And she certainly had after his vote of confidence.

She would float on that warm glow his words had given her as long as she could, and celebrate the success she'd found in her career, especially with the RMKU. She sang a few songs to Nell as she drove, allowing GPS to guide her up through

Moran Junction and the south entrance to Yellowstone. She stopped at the gate and flashed her credentials, explaining she was on official business. The ranger didn't require her to pay the park fee.

Inside the park, she continued along a two-lane highway, slowing in places where buffalo grazed near the road and sometimes on the road. She spotted bull moose way too close for comfort. They were much bigger than she'd thought.

The steering wheel suddenly felt difficult to control, and the Jeep wobbled and pulled to the side. She promptly stopped humming to listen to the unmistakable sound of a flat tire—as if she couldn't already feel it.

Great.

Just great.

She was already arriving at the site later than she'd wanted, as it was. Harlow steered the Jeep to hobble off the main highway toward a connecting forest road. She drove onto the road and parked off to the side to get out of the way. After climbing out, she stretched as she looked around to take in her surroundings. The trees were thick in places and cast long shadows this time of day. Still, it felt peaceful here. She drew in the calming scent of fresh mountain air and pine needles and hoped she wouldn't see bison or moose or, worse, a bear, anywhere nearby.

Maybe her noisy flat tire had scared off the wildlife.

Fine by her.

Hiking around to the passenger side, she confirmed what she already knew.

A flat tire.

Harlow blew out a frustrated breath. Might as well get it over with as soon as possible.

It took her far too long to find what she would need to assemble the jack kit. Seriously? It was stored behind the passenger seat, of all places. Fortunately, the spare tire was hooked to the back of the Jeep— in plain sight. Though the temperature was in the low sixties, she'd worked up a sweat searching for all the tools she'd need to change a flat, and removed her jacket, then laid it in the back seat.

Nell whined in her crate.

"It's okay, girl. I'll get you some water after I finish. You and me both."

Harlow knelt to remove the lug nuts. Crouching, she was breathing hard by the time she got to the last lug nut, then froze.

Had she heard footsteps in the woods behind her?

Not a herd of anything.

A lone creature.

A bear? Buffalo? The larger-than-life moose?

Or…two-footed? She slowly glanced behind her.

And saw nothing. Frowning she continued to watch and listen.

The sooner she changed the tire, the faster she could get out of there. She focused on the tire.

From inside the back of the Jeep, Nell released a low, warning growl, then barked.

Harlow started to stand.

Strong arms gripped her from behind and lifted her off her feet as if to carry her away.

Several blonde women had been abducted from the parks. *Harlow* was a blonde.

She cried out with a gasp while at the same time swinging the lug wrench over her head without thinking. Reflex? Training? She didn't know. Didn't care. She only cared that the heavy wrench connected with her attacker. She wished she'd heard bone cracking.

A masculine yelp resounded in her ears and, with a growl, he released her so that she dropped to the gravel road, landing on her stomach. She twisted around to gain her footing and defend herself if necessary, and also try to identity him, but he was running away, dashing between the trees. He held his arm as he ran. Oh yeah, she'd injured the guy. Scrambling to her feet, Harlow considered giving chase.

Her gun was in her vehicle and should have been on her person. She opened the door and grabbed it, her hands shaking, and held it at the ready in case he came back. He had no idea he'd just attacked a police officer! She pushed down the rising indignation and felt for her badge hanging around her neck on the lanyard.

Remaining next to the Jeep, she scanned the woods. He'd disappeared, and she had no backup or else she would give chase.

She hadn't seen his face, but he'd worn jeans, a hoodie and hiking boots. She quickly called 9-1-1 to report what had happened and ask the dispatcher to also alert the head of the task force, who should already be at the site. Not that she had high hopes the guy would be caught—easily.

This was a national park. Everyone wore jeans, hoodies and hiking boots. No wonder the perp was so hard to find. He fit right in with day hikers and campers. Harlow dusted off the dirt and pine needles, hating that her whole body now trembled. Again, she peered through the trees. She still had a tire to change. Would he come back?

She'd have to be a lot more careful and aware of her surroundings; though she'd heard the footsteps initially, she'd let it go.

Harlow took a deep calming breath and quickened the pace, working past her fumbling, trembling hands. She finished the tire switch-out, finally tightening the last lug on the replacement tire. She didn't bother to repack the jack kit, but instead tossed all the tools next to Nell's crate in the back.

She stuffed the flat tire into the back as well. "Sorry, girl. I'll put it where it goes when we get somewhere safe."

Besides, they'd already lost too much time.

She shoved down the growing frustration—the day had started with such promise.

Then she hopped in, started the Jeep

and steered back onto the highway, leaving the upsetting incident behind her—for now. Had the perp terrorizing blondes across the region been the one who'd just attacked her?

When she finally pulled in behind the vehicles representing several local agencies at the trailhead, relief washed through her. She hopped out and tried to let go of the incident and focus on what came next.

She knew how to do her job and, when she and Nell were working, Harlow was at her best. So she focused on her goal and opened Nell's crate. She assumed the dispatcher had alerted the team leader about her attack and that rangers were currently searching the site. If they found someone suspicious, they'd call in to the group. For now, though, she and Nell needed to get to work. Finding a body would be heartbreaking, but could also lead to the evidence necessary to catch the perp.

Nell harnessed and leashed, they set off on the trail. "Here we go, girl."

A few minutes in, she spotted a law enforcement contingency near the location, according to the coordinates on her GPS, of the site in question. She urged Nell forward toward the others in the woods.

A few of the deputies were much too close to the site.

"Hey, you! Back up. You're too close. What do you think you're doing?" Surely, they knew better than to contaminate the site and evidence. Too late, she realized she'd let the adrenaline still rushing through her after the incident radiate through her tone. Harlow was about to say more when a man who'd had his back to her—and was appropriately not standing too close to the mound of dirt—turned around.

No...

Her past suddenly slammed into her.

FBI Special Agent Wes Grey fought to maintain his composure, though his heart had a mind of its own and pounded painfully against his rib cage. Seeing Harlow Zane here had shocked him.

The trouble was, he couldn't figure out if this was a good thing or a bad thing. And even the fact that he was confused about his reaction to her astonished him. Actually, his reaction felt more like the shock of the earth rolling beneath his feet. But he kept his face emotionless, his astonishment hidden away. At the FBI academy, he and Harlow had been rivals, and it hadn't ended well.

She lifted her lanyard, holding up her badge. "I'm Officer Harlow Zane with the Rocky Mountain K-9 Unit, and this is Nell. Please move back." She let her piercing gaze flick to him briefly. "All of you."

Okay, then. Everyone obeyed as the feisty K-9 handler took charge of the site. Yep. Harlow Zane hadn't changed from the spirited woman he'd known. She was dressed in plain clothes, the lanyard with badge and her gun in the holster at her waist setting her apart as law enforcement. The dog wore a K-9 uniform.

Fighting the smile that wanted to emerge, he kept his expression straight and serious.

Harlow unleashed her cadaver-detection beagle. "Time to work, Nell." She rubbed the dog's neck and gave a command to search. "Find Trudy."

The phrase surprised him, but he knew some handlers preferred creating a more sensitive command for their dogs than "find the dead body."

Wagging her tail, the K-9 went right to work, sniffing around the site.

Harlow hadn't acted as though she'd recognized Wes, all but ignoring him. Then again, their falling out had happened eight years ago and maybe she had forgotten him altogether. She was still beautiful and quite the professional. He'd been impressed with her skills at the academy and today he remained impressed with her take-charge attitude, though she'd taken on quite a different role than an FBI special agent.

After a few minutes and the dog hadn't detected anything, Harlow glanced up at the trees, the group watching, then finally looked directly at Wes. "There's no decomposing body in the ground here."

"Thank you, Officer Zane, for your and Nell's assistance." Wes directed his next words to the sheriff. "Go ahead and have your evidence team overturn the ground in case they find clues to help in the search for the missing park ranger."

Wes worked out of the Cheyenne, Wyoming, office—for now, at least—and had been tapped to head up this task force. He'd flown into Jackson this morning once they'd located what was believed to be a possible grave, after park ranger Cassidy Leidel had gone missing.

The task force team included several agencies in addition to the FBI: park rangers, National Park Service ISB—Investigative Services Branch—and the local sheriff's office, along with its evidence-recovery team. The locals were well equipped, so it would be up to Wes to decide if the FBI's ERT—Evidence Response Team—was required. At some point, if needed, he would bring them in. But for now, the county technicians would overturn the ground.

While he gave them space to work, he stood back and watched. The disturbed ground was shallow and it only took a few minutes to unearth the obvious remains of a campsite: charred wood and ash, food wrappers, a ripped bandanna and a piece of a leather boot lace.

But no body, confirming what Nell had already told them on her search. He hadn't expected to find one.

"Bag the items," he said, knowing they could still be useful and serve as evidence in case the plot of ground ended up being part of their investigation. After all, someone had gone to the trouble to completely cover up their tracks because this wasn't a registered or authorized campsite. At the moment, Wes and the team couldn't know if the reasons were more nefarious.

He couldn't banish the sense that coming up empty-handed here felt like the task force had wasted time. Wes fisted his hands in frustration. The sheriff's evidence team, deputies and rangers began clearing out, though some lingered, keeping their voices low so Wes couldn't hear their conversation. He couldn't care less about their discussion.

Because...unfortunately, every moment spent unearthing the mound, Wes had remained aware of Harlow's presence. Her beauty and skills. After Nell had completed the failed search, Harlow had given the K-9 a reward. Her soft voice drifted over to him while she conversed with a deputy and park staff, who, apparently, had been given permission to pet the dog.

Of course, Wes needed to talk to the handler he'd requested via the RMKU, but it was Harlow, and he was having trouble mustering...what? The courage? His mouth went dry and cottony at the thought of talking to Harlow for the first time in years. As head of this task force, he couldn't afford to be anything other than professional, and while such behavior wasn't like him to begin with, he hadn't expected to see her ever again.

He was still trying to recover from the fact that Harlow Zane, his old academy rival, was here and now on this task force. He shook his head at the strange way that life worked out sometimes. Harlow had been much more than an academy rival. Much. Much. More.

But Wes's ambition and drive, his willingness to be creative when it came to bending the rules, had destroyed the potential romantic relationship they might have had. At least, he'd always thought that had been the reason whatever it was they'd had between them had imploded.

Back then, Harlow Zane had taken his breath away. And watching her now, nothing much had changed in that regard because his breath hitched as the memories flooded him.

At the academy, they'd been opposites when it came to working together, and he had blown it on their training exercise. Their falling out had made him realize he hadn't had the time to nurture a relationship or to fall in love while he was working to become the best agent he could. What had happened with her had almost cost him his dream of becoming a special agent. And then, once he'd started working for the FBI, he'd resolved that a relationship would only be a distraction that would get in the way of his career aspirations. He wouldn't let that happen.

Harlow was alone now, petting Nell, then standing and walking away from the site, toward the trail. He would think she would at least acknowledge him as the head of the task force and head right for him. That told him she hadn't gotten over what had happened any more than he had.

But he'd come to realize the burden of eight years ago lay on his shoulders and it was now up to him to take the first step to smooth things over.

He'd almost caught up to Harlow and thought to call after her, but hesitated. What was holding him back?

Stay on task, man.

"Harlow, wait up, please," he called as he hurried forward, his steps silent as he walked on pine needles.

Her shoulders stiffened but she continued to walk—or was Nell pulling her along?—as if she hadn't heard.

But Wes wouldn't be deterred. He sidled up next to her where the trail allowed, noting his presence hadn't startled her. Yeah, she knew he'd called out to her.

"Harlow, I need to speak with you, please."

She pulled Nell back to her and crouched to hug her dog. He followed suit, squatting to let the dog sniff his hand, making quick friends with her. He'd love to hear about what had landed Harlow as a handler in a K-9 unit, but with the many K-9 units available in this region of the country, he was surprised that their worlds had collided yet again. Likely, Harlow didn't have that answer either.

An awkward silence filled the air and words caught in Wes's throat. She finally stood and, as he also rose, he snagged her blue-eyed gaze and held on. Memories aside, he admitted nothing had changed about his reaction to her—he could look at her eyes forever.

But they had work to do.

Say something.

"I'm excited to have you on the task force."

"Did you..."

Though she didn't finish the sentence, he could read the question in her eyes. She was asking if he'd personally picked her.

"No. I contacted my SAC—Special Agent in Charge—who requested that Tyson Wilkes send someone from the

RMKU. But I know he couldn't have sent a better law enforcement officer." He might have sounded like a blubbering idiot, but his words were true. "I have full confidence in you and Nell, but I also have a concern. A couple of them, actually."

He paused while the sheriff and a few of his deputies hauled shovels back toward the trail and came within earshot. When they were well away, he continued. "First, yes, we've had our differences in the past, but I know that we can put everything behind us and work together to find a killer before he strikes again. We're both professionals with years of experience under our belts now."

He wanted to prove a point to them both—they could work together professionally without a hitch. Blowing it here as opposed to the academy could cost their careers, though he had already turned down a big promotion to work at the Wyoming field office when his mother had had a stroke a few months ago.

Harlow arched a brow as if she thought he was speaking the words for his own benefit as well. Maybe he was. Or maybe she was expecting an apology. She had a right to expect that and he should say he was sorry about what happened before. But this didn't seem like the right moment.

He couldn't tell what she was thinking.

Then she nodded and said, "Agreed. And what else concerns you?"

She'd said she agreed, but in her eyes, he thought he read another message there entirely—that she wasn't sure they could work together. But he should stop second-guessing what she was thinking.

"I'm not sure what you know about the case," he said.

Harlow didn't even blink. Did she already know? Or was she just that good at self-control and hadn't wanted him to see her react? To spot any weakness that could give him a reason to send her away. He didn't want a reason to send her away, did he?

"You think I could be a target," she finally said.

Because with her blond hair and blue eyes, Harlow looked like all the victims.

"You fit the description." Perfectly.

"I know," she said. "And I have no doubt the killer already tried to abduct me."

He stared at her. "*What?*"

She told him about the attempted kidnapping while changing a flat. The report hadn't gotten back to him. In thirty seconds, he'd be on the phone with Dispatch and whoever they'd relayed her call to. Right now, he needed to make sure Harlow was all right.

"I didn't hear that yet. I'm sorry. Are you okay?"

How could she be?

"I'll be okay. We have a job to do. And I'm going to do mine."

TWO

A sliver of fear spread through Harlow, but she shoved it away as he wrapped up his calls with the dispatcher and his team. Rangers had been sent to the attack site, but they'd found no one suspicious. No surprise there.

He walked back over, looking grim.

"Do you know how many blond-haired, blue-eyed women there are, even in this park?" she asked. "I'm not saying I wasn't a target or that it wasn't the perp who'd grabbed me, but we can't be sure either." She'd hoped that stating that fact would make her feel better. It didn't.

Wes looked away for a moment. "We can't be sure of anything. You didn't see his face?"

She shook her head. "I wish I had. As I said, I did injure him, though. His arm. We could check clinics and hospital records for a recently broken humerus."

He nodded. "Already put someone on that." He stared at her. "You will remain alert, right?"

His words grated across her nerves. He'd said it like she wasn't going to remain watchful. The muscles in her neck tensed, but she kept her cool when she said, "I'm always alert." She sounded defensive, so maybe not so much.

Heart pounding, she forced herself to remain calm and confident when she looked in those intense eyes. Gray, like his last name. She held back a silly, bubbly laugh that almost escaped.

Seriously. She'd prepared herself for this assignment, but she hadn't been prepared to see her ex again; the man who'd played a role in her past failure.

Special Agent Wes Grey. With his ambition, she'd have thought he'd be overseeing some big field office by now. But she wouldn't bring that up. Just over six feet tall, he was slender and sinewy, and his light brown hair rustled with the breeze coming down off the mountain. It brought with it the scent of pine along with the odor of geothermal activity. She pressed the back of her hand against her nose to stave off the stink of sulfur as she took in this special agent man. And, yes, he was very special.

He looked too good in a suit. Much too good.

"I hadn't meant to suggest otherwise." Wes suddenly averted his gaze. Interesting. And unexpected. "I want to make sure everyone on my team is safe, especially someone who's already been targeted."

Harlow shrugged. "I'll be vigilant." Panic coiled around her insides and squeezed. There was no way she'd let him send her away just because she matched the perp's MO of choosing blonde, blue-eyed women. She could hold her own against the guy—and on the task force.

This was her big chance to bring closure to families and make a difference. Plus, it could open up other doors for her and Nell. Besides...even if she became a target again, it wouldn't preclude them from catching this guy, and she wanted to be part of the team to stop him from hurting more women. Since she looked like all the victims, maybe she could be used as bait.

Wes cleared his throat and she glanced at him.

"What are you thinking?"

Oh, nothing, really. I'm thinking it's getting late and I'm tired and hungry. She absolutely couldn't tell him what she was thinking because that, too, could give him reason to replace her. Harlow stared up at the tree canopy. Dusk would be on them soon. And they both stood there as if they didn't know how to be around each other anymore. True. So true. But they would have to remedy that and fast.

"I need to get Nell settled."

His smile disarmed her, and she let herself relax with him. Just a little.

"Follow me—" he gestured "—and I'll show you to the accommodations I've arranged for the task force. Some members are local. Some are coming from a distance. We'll be staying at a lodge near Old Faithful."

"That sounds like a plan." She'd packed a bag in case she was invited to stay, sure, but she hadn't known Wes Grey was in charge, much less that he would be here in Wyoming and staying in the *same* lodge. Incredulity rolled through her. What else could possibly happen to throw her off?

The uncomfortable silence between them continued as they hiked down the trail until they made it to the trailhead and their vehicles. Harlow was thankful when Wes left her and approached the sheriff to speak with him. Relief whooshed through her at his departure. She'd get a few minutes to herself to gather her composure, which she hadn't had since first seeing him. She'd tried to ignore him when everyone had started exiting the alleged grave-turned-covert-campsite, but he'd followed her. Yeah…she should have known he would. And, really, she should have been the one to approach him.

In the moments after Nell had failed to alert on the site, Harlow's professionalism had been seriously lacking. But she could do this—work with Wes.

"Come on, girl. It's been a long day. I need to get you fed." Nell licked Harlow's face.

"Yeah, and I'm hungry too." She loaded Nell into her crate in the back, wishing she'd had a chance to put the tire where it belonged. And she certainly wasn't going to do that now in front of Wes.

She quietly groaned at herself. Really. Why should she care if he saw her or not?

Except…well, he might ask questions and she wasn't sure she wouldn't squirm under his intense gaze, and she might end up telling him her idea about using herself as bait. She wasn't even sure of that yet herself—and telling him might get her sent packing for "her own protection."

She rubbed Nell's head, then shut the crate. "It won't be long now before we get to go to bed. I'm tired too."

Nell wagged her tail and then curled up in the crate.

"I feel the same way." Harlow couldn't wait for the moment she went to bed in a quiet room all to herself. Exhaustion from the long day of travel weighed on her, then the attempted abduction and the struggle, and then seeing Wes at the site had jarred her, draining her even more.

"You ready?" His sudden appearance behind her startled her. She'd had enough of that.

She swallowed against the tightness in her throat, closed the back of the Jeep quickly before he could see inside, then whirled around and smiled. "Yes. Nell is in her crate. Let's go."

Frowning, he stared into the rear of the Jeep. "I'll make sure your tire is replaced and the spare put back."

"I appreciate that," she said.

The way he studied her, she could tell he was dying to ask questions about the struggle with the attacker, but there was nothing more to report. She suspected he was assessing if she were about to fall apart, which she clearly wasn't.

Harlow had always had to work harder, it seemed, to prove herself. Friends had told her that she was beautiful, and that somehow misled certain people to underestimate her. In this day and age, it seemed abominable. But Wes knew her well enough, and that wasn't where he was coming from. She had to be misreading him and letting the chip on her shoulder come into play here. At least she could admit that much—to herself, of course.

"Yeah, me too." She climbed into the Jeep, shut the door, then lowered the window. "I'm ready to follow you to the lodge."

He nodded and made his way over to his black Suburban. She waited for him to steer onto the road and then she followed, keeping pace with his vehicle until they turned into the Old Faithful Visitor Education Center, drove through the parking lot and over to a huge rustic lodge that looked like a log cabin castle.

He waited for her to get out of her vehicle and secure Nell, but neither of them said much. What had happened before still hung in the air between them. For the life of her, she didn't know how to clear things up and move on.

Lord, help me get past the resentment and anger. It was all still there, festering in her heart all these years, and she hadn't even realized it.

Fortunately, she wouldn't have to eat dinner with him or talk to him because he answered a call and disappeared.

She breathed a sigh of relief and grabbed a sandwich to go, compliments of the lodge to the task force members, and settled into her woodsy accommodations—a small bedroom decorated to complement the rustic lodge. She'd left Nell's crate in the Jeep for tonight, and the beagle curled up on the round braided rug, featuring bears, that covered the wood floor.

Harlow tugged out her laptop and Bible and chose to read for a while, a soft lamp by the bed lighting the pages. Then she settled in to sleep. Tomorrow would be a long day, and she had no idea what to expect.

Serving on the RMKU was one thing, but this task force business was next level. She intended to hit every mark and hoped and prayed she and Wes wouldn't be at odds like they'd been at the academy—at least at the end. The awful…terrible end.

Tucking the pillow under her, she closed her eyes, expecting exhaustion to send her right to sleep.

But she heard a voice coming through the wall from the room next to hers. Really?

Oh. And, of course, she recognized that voice.

Wes was on the phone again.

Come on. Why did he have to be right next door? She turned to her side and punched the pillow as thoughts about her shouting at him after that failed exercise at the academy came back to her. Everyone watching. *Everyone.* Their superiors too. That incident had changed her future.

She had to let it go. And focusing on finding a killer was exactly the kind of case she needed to let the past go.

Stop the madness.

She had a feeling that it was easier said than done. Their careers and their hearts had been wrapped up in what had gone wrong.

Sheer exhaustion finally pulled her under into a fitful sleep.

Harlow woke to her alarm and she yawned and stretched. Hard to believe she had finally fallen asleep. She took Nell outside for a short walk then, after she'd showered and dressed, grabbed a quick breakfast. Wes had arranged for the task force to meet in a small conference room at the lodge.

Harlow showed up with Nell and saw some of the same people who had been at the disturbed plot of ground yesterday.

Wes began the meeting with official introductions, making sure to welcome Harlow as the newest member. "We met at the FBI academy, and I know she and Nell are a vital addition to our team."

Wes cleared his throat, then continued. "Let's start with what we know," Wes said. "There have been four victims— four women—abducted from across the region. All blonde, blue-eyed and in their twenties. Emery Rodgers was the first taken. She was in New Mexico and her body was found strangled. Then Brittany Albradt in Colorado, Valentina Silva in Utah and Elena Kimball over the border in Wyoming. All missing. So far, we've only found Emery's body. All four women were doing outdoor activities like hiking, biking or camping when they disappeared." He turned to plot the locations on the map behind him. "Now, we believe that our perp has struck again. Park ranger Cassidy Leidel has gone missing, having been last seen yesterday at the Old Faithful Backcountry ranger station in Yellowstone National Park."

Wes continued by handing out the tasks for various team members. "We can't be one hundred percent certain that Cassidy Leidel's disappearance has anything to do with our case, but with her blond hair and blue eyes, she fits the description of all the victims. And given that she was in uniform, the perp is getting more brazen."

Wes's gaze flicked over to Harlow, lingered, before moving on. She was sure others in the room had noticed.

"As you all know now, Officer Zane was attacked while changing a flat tire on her way to the site yesterday. She wasn't in uniform, but she certainly fits the description of the victims. Thanks to her training and quick thinking, she was able to get away, but the perp disappeared. Again, we can't be sure it's our guy, but there's a very good chance it is. Everyone needs to be on red alert. Particularly Officer Zane."

As eyes swung to her again, Harlow couldn't help the heat that rose to her cheeks. Once again, when it came to Wes, she couldn't seem to maintain her self-control.

She excused herself from the room early, claiming an important call from her unit. The meeting was nearly over anyway, and better she was out here, reining in her lack of control over her emotions, than for everyone to see her overreaction.

Wes hiked toward her, and she turned her back on him as if she hadn't seen him. She was blowing this all by herself. No help from him at all.

"What was that about?" He had an edge to his tone.

She bristled. Breathed through her nostrils. Slow and steady. But she couldn't respond yet.

"We don't need theatrics, Harlow."

Oh. Wow. Had he really just said that? And just like she'd thought, the air between them had not been cleared. He still remembered everything in detail—apparently—and so did she. She took a long, deep breath. She had no choice but to face him.

She dreaded looking into his eyes—she might see how disappointed he was.

In her.

Wes held back what more he might have said. In fact, he'd said too much already, letting their past creep into this situation—and he'd resolved he wouldn't do that. Here he was, doing just that. But those academy memories of their confrontation in front of their peers and superiors weren't so easily set aside, especially with the way that Harlow reacted today. Of course, he was the only one in the room to read her actions that way. Everyone else thought Harlow had needed to take a call. But Wes knew better. She hadn't been on the phone when he'd gone after her. And he'd seen the slight coloring in her face and the flash of anger in her eyes.

Anger directed at him. He'd seen that same flash of fire when she'd exploded at him years ago, not caring that others were looking on. She'd had no self-control. The drama of their confrontation had played out in a worst-case scenario and had nearly cost him his dream. He couldn't let her "theatrics" happen again or it could unravel this task force. He'd already taken a detour on his career path—deliberate, of course, to be close for Mom—and heading up this task force had been just what he'd needed, a confirmation of sorts that his superiors still believed in him. He'd get his chance to oversee a field office— one day.

But not if Harlow derailed both their careers. Still, he needed to act the leader here, to model a professional and calm attitude. Not unload on her. Wes drew in several long, calming breaths. She had skills and experience, too, and really...her leaving the space to take a breather had probably been a wise decision. He shouldn't be so hard on her. Yeah. He was the one overreacting now.

He blew out a breath, allowing all the tension to dissipate. Wes would give Harlow the benefit of a doubt. Give her a chance to explain why she'd left so abruptly—so he wouldn't second-guess her thoughts. He needed to know what was going on in that head of hers so they could be a cohesive team.

Harlow looked everywhere except at Wes. He fisted his hands.

Then, finally, she angled her beautiful face and striking blue eyes at him and locked on, holding his gaze. He couldn't look away if he wanted to and, for some reason, he had the sudden urge to protect his deepest thoughts from her searching eyes.

"Listen, Wes, we've got to work together

on this," she said. "So, for our victims' sakes, let's just pretend we have no past."

He should be the one saying those words to her. Putting the past behind them was the only way. "My sentiments exactly."

Considering his reaction this morning, he had to admit that would be impossible for him, especially since so much more had happened between them than a falling out. They'd dated and he'd cared deeply for her, but at the time, it had become clear they could never be together.

Forcing a smile, he tried to smooth the frown out of his face. He felt that smile, he really did, somewhere deep inside. "Our past forgotten, I'd like you and Nell to accompany me today."

Her eyes widened. She hadn't expected that one. Neither had he.

Her expression was tenuous at first, then warmer. "Okay. Where are we going?"

"To search the ranger station and Cassidy Leidel's cabin to see if Nell detects any scents that could tell us something."

"You're talking residual. Decomposing parts, including blood or tissue."

"You got it. If she was killed and the killer moved her elsewhere, Nell can still identify the scent of death in the area, can't she?"

"Definitely. Plus, she can differentiate between animals and humans, but you probably already knew that. She can find scents deep in the ground or under collapsed buildings." Harlow knelt next to her beagle to run her fingers through her fur, clearly proud of her dog. And her feelings went deeper than mere admiration—she obviously loved Nell as well. The two had a special relationship.

Special relationship.

He'd once had that with Harlow.

Shoving the unbidden thought aside, he focused on the present. Their mission to save lives.

"Now that you and Nell are here, I don't want to waste any time. If she can find a scent, then we can locate the killer at large. We can stop him…or her…from killing. And we can bring closure to families. At the same time, we're still holding out hope that Cassidy is still alive out there somewhere." And for that reason alone, he hoped that Nell didn't alert to anything.

Harlow's expression was grim. "But she's a skilled ranger and could at least radio for help to let someone know she was hurt or injured. And if she was unconscious…it's been too long."

"So it doesn't look good, and that's why you're here with Nell." He hated saying the words.

Harlow's beautiful blue eyes brightened with his words, as if he'd struck an internal chord. He'd like to know what that was about. Then again, he should steer clear of too many personal conversations that could stir up an emotional connection. He already knew he was susceptible when it came to Harlow.

"The ranger station is also the visitor education center." He pointed to the south.

"It's that large cabin across the parking lot and up the path. Are you and Nell good to walk there?"

"Always." She rose to stand. "Lead the way. We're ready."

Once they were at the ranger station/visitor center, Harlow gave Nell the command to search, but kept her on the leash so the visitors wouldn't be startled or disturbed by a beagle sniffing around. While Harlow worked with Nell, Wes secured the key to Cassidy's cabin from her supervisor and planned to return to ask more questions.

He found Harlow and Nell peering at a rack of postcards featuring the Old Faithful geyser, buffalo and all manner of wildlife and nature settings.

"Well?" He asked the question though he already knew the answer.

"Nell didn't alert to anything." Harlow spoke in a hushed tone.

She didn't need to explain the rest, especially here where someone might overhear the conversation. But not alerting meant that Nell hadn't found blood or human tissue. While Wes would prefer finding Cassidy Leidel alive, he couldn't help but be disappointed. The sooner they found clues, the faster they could get the killer.

"What next?" Harlow asked.

"Let's check her cabin. For that, we'll need to take a vehicle." He started toward the parking lot.

Harlow and Nell kept pace with him, though his legs were much longer. Maybe he should slow down a bit.

"We'll take mine then. Nell's crate is in the back."

"Along with the flat tire. I called a garage about that this morning, as I said I would, but it might be a while. Just trying to help." A friend in need, though he wasn't sure they were even to friend status at the moment.

He caught the amusement in her eyes. "The spare should hold up for today. We have to find Cassidy Leidel. You don't want to waste time, remember?"

He held his palms up in surrender. "You're absolutely right."

At her Jeep, she secured Nell in the crate, and he climbed into the passenger side. When she got in, he directed her to Cassidy's cabin, which was two miles up the road and off the beaten path. She steered along the bumpy not-even-a-road and parked away from the cabin so they wouldn't disturb possible evidence.

"It looks kind of like a backcountry off-grid sort of tourist accommodation," she said.

"Sometimes the rangers live in them during certain seasons. I wouldn't think she would stay here in the winter, but what do I know?"

Harlow instructed Nell to search the wooded area before they reached the cabin. After all, if the ranger was killed here, her body could even be in these woods around her cabin, though it was likely the area had already been searched.

"The ranger probably felt connected to nature out here."

Wes didn't point out that Nell was even now searching for her dead body, but he'd understood what Harlow meant. Somehow, in all of this, they held on to the slightest hope that Cassidy wasn't dead.

Nell finally led them to Cassidy's cabin. Wes unlocked and opened the door, standing back to watch Nell search the cabin. Then, wearing gloves, Wes riffled through papers on a small desk to see if something clued him in as to why the ranger had gone missing.

The dog finally sat at Harlow's feet…a nonsignal.

Wes looked from the desk to Harlow.

She shook her head. "Nell didn't detect any scents that would indicate a dead body."

"Cassidy wasn't killed here then." He sighed. "Why don't you have Nell search in a wider circle in the woods? I'll go with you. Let's start again near the cabin."

"But..." Harlow pursed her lips, then said, "Okay. We're going back outside, Nell."

"I know you already searched the area, but we can go wider."

She nodded but said nothing. He suspected she was thinking that Nell would detect the scent for more than a mile, so what was the point. But he wasn't ready to give up. And while the K-9 searched again, Wes focused on locating clues outside the cabin. He was rewarded when he found boot prints under Cassidy's window. He knelt and wished he had a casting kit. But he didn't have his vehicle.

On his cell, he requested the task force evidence tech, Bill Wilhite from the county sheriff's department, come to the cabin. Then Wes slowly joined Harlow and Nell as they spread their search parameters in the wooded area away from the cabin.

After a good half hour, Harlow turned

to Wes. "If she was murdered, then she was killed somewhere else. But at least you found a clue."

"Yeah. The prints under the window could mean someone was peering into the window. They're large, so probably belong to a man and not Cassidy herself."

"So she was being watched?" Harlow let Nell lead them, sniffing her way back to the Jeep.

"And if so, did he come back for her? Let's wait here for the evidence tech to cast those prints. Shouldn't be too long now."

He'd barely finished speaking when a county utility vehicle drove up and parked behind Harlow's Jeep. Deputy Perry Heigl accompanied Bill, who carried the casting kit. Good. He hadn't come alone. It was best they all continued to work in teams for everyone's safety.

Wes showed them the boot prints and then left them to it. Back in Harlow's Jeep, he rubbed his temples while he thought through their next steps.

"We should probably grab some lunch." Her soft voice broke through his thoughts. "I need to get Nell some water. For September, it's sure warm."

"I couldn't agree more."

She started the engine and turned the Jeep around to leave behind Cassidy's cabin.

"You and Nell are probably the most valuable assets on this task force."

She said nothing as she stopped at the intersection of the unpaved cabin road and the state highway. "Where to?"

"I want you with me as I look into anyone who had contact with Cassidy over the past few days. Nell could alert to something. Right now, let's head back to the Old Faithful area and grab some lunch, then to the ranger station. I want to talk to her supervisor about her last few days. I got the key from him, but he wasn't able to talk."

"Thank you, by the way," she said. "For

what you said earlier about Nell and me. I appreciate that. It means a lot to me and, I'm sure, to Nell too. We're happy to join you, and if there's something to find, Nell will find it."

"I have no doubt." He was laying it on too thick, but he believed the words.

Once again, he heard the intense pride she had in Nell, her cadaver dog, and he wanted to know how she'd gone from the FBI academy to being a K-9 handler.

Eight years ago, he'd resolved that he would never again let someone distract him from his career path. Okay, well, Mom's stroke had put a kink in that track… But Harlow hadn't been part of that close family circle. Then why had he never stopped wishing things could have been much different between them?

THREE

Harlow wasn't sure what to think about her reaction to Wes's praise. Warmth flooded out of her heart all the way to her toes. Seriously—why did it matter so much what he thought of her? Sure, he was the head of the task force and his praise meant everything in terms of her career, but she knew it was much more than that. She cared what Wes thought about her, regardless of her career aspirations. Pathetic.

And what was with the now-familiar uncomfortable silence that grew between them as she drove them to the ranger station? If they were going to be working together as much as he'd alluded to, then she would have to find a way to make conversation or be comfortable in the silence.

Maybe some redirection would remedy the awkwardness. "So…have you gotten any word through the FBI grapevine about the missing baby?"

He lowered his window about halfway, letting in the breeze. "Chloe Baker?"

She nodded. Like everyone at the RMKU, Harlow prayed that the little girl would be located. Several months ago, a car had been found ablaze near Rocky Mountain National Park, a woman unconscious nearby—along with an empty baby seat and a baby blanket. But the baby had never been found. The team's investigation had led to the driver's identity—Kate Montgomery—and she'd recently woken from her coma but had no memory of the accident or who would want to hurt her. She wasn't the mother of the missing baby.

In fact, the mother, Nikki Baker, had been found dead in her own vehicle in a ditch not too far away from the crime scene. Now in rehab, Kate was working with a memory specialist, but so far, she couldn't tell the team anything they hadn't uncovered through their investigation. The names—Nikki and Chloe Baker—were familiar to Kate, but she couldn't recall why the baby might have been in her car in the first place.

The RMKU's work on Nikki Baker's possible homicide wasn't turning up any solid leads either. A very expensive watch had been found in her apartment with initials that no one could tie to her. Harlow had always thought those initials were key.

"I know the FBI had theorized about the possibility of a baby smuggling ring in the region, but it's slow going." He shook his head. "I hope little Chloe is all right, wherever she is."

Me, too, she thought, trying to refocus on the case at hand. She steered into the Old Faithful hydrothermal site and drove past the ranger station. "We're getting lunch, right?"

"Yes." Wes seemed a little tense. She was too.

She parked near the lodge. A crowd of tourists had gathered around the Old Faithful geyser, waiting for it to shoot up into the air at any moment. The gathering wasn't nearly as big as she'd imagined it would be during the summer months, but September was cooler and less crowded—a great time to visit the park. If she ever came back this way again and wasn't working on an investigation, she'd love to explore the supervolcano called Yellowstone. One of nature's most spectacular wonders—she was beginning to see that now.

She turned off the Jeep and lowered her window. A cool breeze drifted inside. The day had grown warm, but the air held a hint of the colder months to come. Nell whined in the back. Harlow hopped out and went around to open the hatch. She offered Nell some water.

Wes lingered nearby, staring at the geyser now blowing hot steam and water into the air. Even from this distance, the crowd could be heard oohing and aahing.

Harlow couldn't stop thinking about the missing baby. Chloe Baker's mother was dead, and her father was unknown, but someone had to be missing that little girl. Harlow understood the need to know what happened when a loved one went missing…after the gruesome discovery that had changed the course of her life. Even though she'd only been twelve. Of course, she'd needed therapy for a few years to deal with the trauma of that day.

Wes had fully turned his back on her now, facing the crowd surrounding nature's grand display. Was he hoping to spot the killer among the tourists?

She bent to leash Nell and let her out of the Jeep. She hadn't wanted her thoughts to go there, but she couldn't close the floodgate that had been opened.

All because she'd cared about that still-missing baby.

Her heart ached at the thought. Law enforcement did their best to serve and protect, and yes, to find people who went missing, but sometimes it wasn't enough. Sometimes mistakes were made.

At the academy, she and Wes had been paired up to resolve a mock hostage situation. Together they had laid out the plans for rescuing an abducted woman. But Wes had improvised and hadn't followed their plan at all, and in the end, they'd failed to save the hostage. An overachiever—just like Wes—that failure had cut Harlow to the core. She'd been barely relieved it was only an exercise and not real life. Regardless of how the incident had impacted her emotionally and personally, it had been a mark against them both.

And what had come next was all on her.

She'd gone on a blasting tirade, telling him what she'd truly thought about him. That he was impulsive and inconsiderate of others. That, in the future, people would die because of him. And the look on his face at her crushing words...

Harsh. Truly harsh. Not only had her outburst obliterated a budding relationship, she'd lost control in front of everyone and had been humiliated. She'd never fully recovered from that day and was glad when, after graduation, an opportunity had opened up for her to join the Santa Fe PD. She would be closer to her family, but more than that, she'd needed a fresh start.

She'd wanted to forget about the FBI, at least the academy. And she'd wanted to forget about Wes Grey, but he had remained at the back of her thoughts until yesterday when she'd seen him again for the first time in years. Now he was at the forefront of her thoughts for all the right reasons.

And all the wrong ones too.

"Earth to Harlow."

Harlow blinked and suddenly realized Wes had not only turned to her, he was standing next to her, too close for comfort, his gray eyes steely and penetrating, as if he could read her mind. She shuddered at the thought that he might so easily learn what she'd been thinking about him and all that had gone wrong. And, yes, some of what had been right...so right during her brief time with him before that life-altering day. She'd worked hard to put it all behind her and now...eight years, five months and ten days later...

She was working for Wes, in a manner of speaking. With him. For him. What difference did it make?

"You were seriously lost in thought. In fact, maybe you still are. Care to share?"

Not a chance. "Let's grab a quick lunch and then talk to Cassidy's supervisor."

Wes's smile reminded her of the good times they'd had, too, before their falling out in the most spectacular way. She instantly warmed to his smile like she always had. She absolutely could not let him get under her skin this time and would remain wary of his changing up the game plan in the middle of the action.

The last thing they needed was to fail to catch a killer.

* * *

After egg salad sandwiches, Wes led Harlow back out to the lodge parking lot. During lunch, they'd talked about the case and a few other investigations, but nothing at all personal. They'd agreed to forget the past, but that agreement seemed to stir up the memories in his mind all the more. Or maybe it was just looking at her face, watching her familiar expressions and quirks that he'd grown to love—back then. Still, their conversation had felt more like a dance around what was really on both of their minds.

But, honestly, he didn't know what was on her mind, and it would be a total guess if he thought he did. She obviously hadn't wanted to share her thoughts, so he should mind his own business and keep up the dance for as long as it took.

Outside, he breathed in the crisp September air, the sulfuric odor that he'd come to associate with Yellowstone.

Wes gestured to the Suburban he'd

rented. "Let's drive instead of walk. It'll save time in case we learn something. We can head out right away."

He hoped they would learn something but, unfortunately, investigations took far longer than portrayed on television crime dramas. That was too bad, too, because more lives could be lost before they stopped this killer.

Harlow nodded. "I agree."

With the way she said the words, he had the feeling that she was eager to be rid of him. The sooner they wrapped up their day, and really, the investigation, the sooner Harlow wouldn't have to see him again.

She paused. "But Nell's crate is in my Jeep. We can just take that, unless for some reason you need to drive."

"Let's move her crate until we get your tired fixed. I think we're pushing it to keep driving on the spare. You don't want to get stuck out here with two flat tires." Wes might have been overstepping. But he spoke the truth.

Harlow angled her head. She'd secured her hair in a ponytail and the look she gave him sent his mind right back to years ago. They were supposed to forget the past. Hard to do when there was still so much about that time he wanted to remember—against his better judgment. But his mind didn't always want to listen to the heart.

And yeah...his heart remembered a lot. The feel of her in his arms, for one thing. He inwardly groaned and clamped down on the flow of memories. Enough.

He cleared his throat and lifted his hands in surrender. "Your call."

But was it really? Who was in charge here anyway?

"I suppose you're right." She opened the hatch and together they moved the dog crate over to his rental Suburban.

Finally, they headed across the parking lot and into another lot next to the ranger station.

He waited for Harlow to retrieve Nell. "Do you take her everywhere with you?"

"When I'm on an investigation, yes."

"Will she alert without a specific command."

"Sometimes. I'm sure you've heard the fact that dogs have about 300 million olfactory receptors in their noses. Now compare that to 6 million for humans. Sure, she's trained on a specific skill, but the rest of it is innate. The difference is that she isn't trained to signal."

"Makes sense."

Harlow smiled and rubbed Nell's head. The dog wagged her tail. "We can communicate though."

"Of that, I have no doubt." He pushed through the visitor center's door and held it open for Harlow and Nell.

Ranger Jonathan Hicks—Cassidy's supervisor—rounded the corner as they entered the main lobby.

Wes made a beeline for him and stopped in the man's path. "Just the person we were looking for."

Hicks was about six feet and in his mid-forties. Had some graying at his temples. His eyes were compassionate though sharp. "Agent Grey. How can I help you?"

All in good time. "This is Officer Harlow Zane with the Rocky Mountain K-9 Unit and Nell. Let's talk in private."

Hicks ushered them out of the main area and down a hallway to a small office. Once they all entered, he shut the door behind them.

Good. The man understood.

"Did you find anything at her cabin?"

"Possibly." Wes would wait to share about the boot prints. "I'd like to hold on to the key to Cassidy's cabin longer, if that's okay." Wes found that people were more likely to cooperate if given the choice.

"Keep it as long as you need it to find her. What else do you need?"

Funny you should ask. "We'd like to look at her schedule for the last few days."

Hicks nodded and opened a drawer in the desk. He pulled out a spiral notebook and set it on the desktop. "This is her logbook. You're welcome to go through it."

"You keep it locked in your desk?" Harlow asked.

"I review the logbooks regularly."

"And you looked through her logbook recently?" Wes kept his tone light.

Hicks pressed his hands against the desk mat and leaned forward. "I did, yes."

"Anything suspicious catch your attention?"

"She had a busy couple of days before her disappearance." The supervisor opened the logbook and pointed to what must be Cassidy's writing. "Here, she notes she took an oversize knife away from a Harrison Cahn." The ranger slid his finger down a few lines and then pressed it on the page again. "She issued a summons to a Martin Barnes for starting an illegal campfire. We have designated fire pits for the campgrounds. Anything outside of those, especially when it's this dry in the park, is just too risky."

"Anything else?" Harlow asked.

Wes noticed Nell sniffing around the office and he remained aware of the beagle. Would she alert to something? And, if so, how would Hicks react?

"Yeah. She warned a guy named David Ellison about vandalism."

"Is vandalism an issue around here?"

"It can be. She didn't leave any details in this case."

"Why do you think that is?"

He shrugged. "I couldn't say."

And now they might not be able to ever ask her.

"If you don't mind," Wes said, "I'll have a look at it too."

Wes reached forward and turned the logbook so he could see.

"And I'll let Nell search again, in case we somehow missed something." Harlow sounded like she doubted that possibility, but he agreed it was a good idea. "Go ahead."

Harlow left the office with Nell so the

beagle could keep looking for evidence of human remains. He both hoped the dog would and wouldn't find it.

Ranger Hicks crossed his arms and leaned against the wall, out of the way.

Wes flipped through the pages and made a mental note of items that caught his attention.

"Anything else you can tell us about Cassidy that might help us find her? Or who might have abducted or killed her?"

"I would have told you already, but that doesn't mean there isn't something I know and forgot or missed. At the moment, nothing comes to mind. But if I think of something, I'll let you know. I want her back with us safe and sound. But with this killer out there..." Hicks shook his head and stared out his office window.

Wes heard the pain and fear in the man's voice, too, and returned his attention to skimming the logbook. He looked at two weeks before the incident and found nothing that stood out. "What did she like to do in her free time?"

The ranger rubbed the back of his neck. "I try to stay out of the private lives of those I supervise. I can say that Cassidy was an extrovert and loved people. What I mean is that she had a soft heart. I can see her stopping to help someone in need and getting into trouble."

"As a park ranger, it would be her job to help someone, isn't that correct?" Wes asked.

"Yes. But Cassidy would be more likely to go out of her way and do more than required."

Wes thought he understood what the supervisor meant. She might make herself vulnerable for someone to take advantage of her.

He closed the logbook. "Please keep this locked in the drawer so we can access it again if we need it." *And possibly take it into evidence.* "Thank you, Ranger Hicks, you've been a lot of help today."

Harlow had re-entered the office and stood behind Wes, Nell at her feet, surprising him.

"You finished already?"

She shrugged. "Nell is done here."

Wes thanked Ranger Hicks again and then followed Harlow and Nell out of the visitor center, stopping a few times for kids to admire the dog.

Once outside, Harlow led Wes over to a porch post and out of earshot of visitors and employees.

By that look in her eyes, he knew she had learned something. "What is it?"

"I spoke with a young woman who is an interpretive park ranger, meaning she leads guided walks around the park, teaches and informs visitors. She'd just come in from guiding some tourists through the geysers around Old Faithful. She stopped to ask about Nell and we started talking. She's very distraught about Cassidy, saying that Cassidy was the one to get her the job here."

"And that's important why?"

"Because before becoming a ranger three years ago, Cassidy worked for the state as a vocational rehabilitation counselor."

Interesting. "What exactly did she do?"

"It sounded like job counseling and referral services, and it included mental rehabilitation."

Wes scratched his jaw. He usually shaved but the scruff on his cheeks confirmed that he'd forgotten this morning. He searched Harlow's eyes and saw those brilliant gears turning. And then he felt it to his bones—he and Harlow were actually working together and…working together well.

He didn't hold back the wry grin. "I see where you're going with this."

She smiled. "Do you?"

"I do. We need to look into anyone whom she might have been rehabilitating or helping on the side, starting with the three men in her logbook."

"And we can start by finding out if any of them fit the profile of a serial killer." Though the task force wouldn't officially call this guy a serial killer until they had found at least one more body, and unfortunately, Wes had a feeling they would and soon.

Dread filled his gut, and he couldn't help that his expression darkened. They knew that *she* fit the description of the victims, and as they closed in on the killer, the danger to Harlow would increase exponentially.

FOUR

Harlow led Nell back to Wes's parked SUV. "How do you suggest we find out if these guys fit the description?"

At his SUV, he opened the back for Harlow to put Nell in her crate. "I noticed that even though Cassidy didn't detail the specific vandalism with David Ellison this time in her logbook, there are several previous entries going back a few weeks."

Interesting. Harlow assisted Nell up into the SUV and then opened the crate. Nell went right in, like she was glad to finally get a chance to rest.

"Good girl." Harlow offered her a treat and some water. "Explain."

"He's a local." Wes studied Harlow.

She caught her breath. "That means…

he's not the guy abducting women all over the Rockies. He's not the man who killed Emery."

"It's not him." He repeated the words, confirming hers. "Our abductor/killer was in Utah during that time."

Harlow rubbed Nell behind the ears, then focused her gaze back on Wes. She recalled seeing him so serious, even at the academy. Emotions rushed through her. "He might not be the man we're searching for, but it's possible that he still kidnapped Cassidy and she isn't a victim of the potential serial killer."

He rubbed his scruffy jaw, his gray eyes studying her. What was he thinking? She thought she might have seen admiration in those eyes, and heat swarmed through her belly. Not good.

"Very perceptive. Her abductor could also be an imitator, except the news media hasn't picked up on the connection yet. I'm hoping to find the perp before we have the potential for a copycat."

Harlow shuddered and rubbed her arms. She glanced over Wes's shoulder and watched the Old Faithful geyser reaching once again to the sky. "I wish I understood why people hurt others."

"If it was a disease, maybe we could cure it." Wes's tone was dark. "Sin. Murder… the first crime against humanity. We're not going to cure it, but we can do our best to stop him from killing again."

His words caught her by surprise. She'd known he was a Christian back at the academy, but he'd never talked about his faith much. Now it was her turn…she couldn't help the admiration that swelled inside.

Wes had been a good man back then, and he was a good man now. She kind of wished she could find something wrong with him…well, other than the past that she blamed him for. And, really, that was on them both. Not just him.

Could she throw the first stone or any stone? No. She wanted to talk about this more, but his cell buzzed.

Disappointment washed over her.

Wes's cell buzzed again and he glanced at it, then hesitated, frowning.

He tucked his cell away and looked at her.

"You're not going to respond?"

"I'll call them back. We need to do some research back at the lodge. I have to make some calls and hear from the rest of the task force. We'll look into the backgrounds of Martin Barnes and Harrison Cahn, and go from there. Nell has done great work today. You both have."

Wes stood there and stared at her, as though gauging her reaction. She was stunned, honestly. He seemed to want to make sure she understood that he appreciated their work.

Who does that?

On the other hand, maybe he was leading up to something...dismissing her from the task force now?

Harlow hated the doubt that crept in. She bit her lip, but part of her felt like he was about to end her time here. "Do you still need our help tomorrow?" *Please...*

"Absolutely."

Relief whooshed through her.

He grinned, that same grin she knew all too well, and it lit heat all the way to her toes. Why did he have to be so...frustrating and adorable at the same time?

"And I didn't tell you," he said. "But that was great work back there, learning about Cassidy's background."

Again, that flood of heat. She hoped he didn't see how his compliments affected her. Still...he was the head of this task force and his assurance meant everything; his support could be invaluable to her career and future. But she shouldn't be thinking about that when lives were at stake and a ranger had likely been killed. The thought soured in her gut.

"What's wrong?"

She stared at the ground. "I hate to think that someone Cassidy was helping abducted her…killed her. That doesn't sound like our killer to me either, unless—"

His cell buzzed again. Wes gently squeezed her shoulder. "Hold that thought. I really need to take this call."

He glanced over at the lodge. Wes had parked as close as he could, but it was still a bit of a hike.

For some reason, Harlow wanted to wait for Wes before heading to the lodge, but she had no reason to. "I'll just take Nell now. We'll walk over to the lodge. She needs the fresh air and exercise."

"You sure?"

She nodded as he answered his cell and stepped away from her.

"Come on, girl." Harlow grabbed Nell and leashed her up. She hoped Wes would remember the crate, but then again, she could work in her room and Nell would just sleep on the rug.

Harlow spent the rest of the afternoon— until she thought her eyes would cross— writing up notes about everything they'd learned so far. Wes had delivered Nell's crate to Harlow's room and informed her the out-of-town task force members staying in the lodge would be meeting for dinner in the dining room at six. She was glad for the news because her stomach had now started growling, and she didn't want to live on vending machine food.

She brought Nell with her and the dog rested at her feet while Harlow concentrated on eating roasted chicken and potato salad, while listening to FBI Special Agent Ricky Shore, out of the Jackson office, and Tanner Adler, a deputy out of Teton County assigned to stick around. Ranger Hicks joined them, too, though he was local. No one talked specifics regarding the investigation because the dining room wasn't private. But Wes had wanted them together to get to know each other and develop a sense of cohesion and camaraderie.

That could only help the investigation. Right?

She hoped they wouldn't be working the case long enough to have cohesion, honestly.

Harlow was relieved when dinner was over and the day was coming to an end. She quickly escaped the group before she got drawn into an activity or discussion—and, really, she needed time away from Wes. The guy was getting under her skin. It was FBI academy all over again. Only this time, there was less of the competitive tension between them and more of a willingness to work together. Maybe life and work experience had something to do with that. They had both come a long way since those days—almost a decade ago. And were different people. Yet he still affected her emotionally. She was drawn to him for reasons she couldn't explain. So, they were different people and yet some things remained the same.

She shook off the thoughts about Wes. Hadn't she wanted to put some distance—mentally and physically—between them?

This was a great time to take Nell for an evening walk. They skirted the main attraction of the Old Faithful geyser and Harlow prayed quietly as she soaked in the beauty of the evergreens and God's amazing creation around her. She could do without the rotten egg smell, though, that permeated the area.

From the path, she spotted Wes in the parking lot. He was about fifty yards away, next to the lodge, talking to Ricky, the other fed about a decade older than Wes, who had mentioned at dinner that he was retiring soon, and that the Jackson office was going to be closed after he left. They must be talking shop.

With his good looks, Wes definitely stood out in a crowd. She zeroed in on his broad shoulders, his athletic form and, though she couldn't see them, she knew that his muscles were sinewy. He kept himself in top form. She really, *really* shouldn't be staring at him or thinking about his physique.

Before she could look away, he glanced at her as though he had some sort of intuition that she'd been watching from a distance. She inwardly groaned. How had he spotted her so easily through the trees? He was out in the open and she was edging the woods.

She ignored Wes and gazed at the geyser. It looked like Old Faithful might spew hot water into the air one more time before dark, and this was her chance to watch nature's display. A small crowd had gathered—not as large as earlier in the day. But she also wanted to avoid Wes—she needed some space. Maybe before she left she'd get the chance to watch the famous geyser's exploits close up. Dogs weren't typically allowed on the boardwalk near Old Faithful unless, of course, they were service dogs. Nell was a working dog, but she wasn't officially working at the moment, and Harlow could tell she was ready to curl up and take a nap as always after her evening walk. But Harlow wanted to see Old Faithful in all its glory.

"Let's get you back to the room, Nell. You got your walk, okay? But I want to see this geyser erupt." Harlow hurried back to her room and got Nell settled in her crate.

She glanced out the window. Ten minutes until the geyser would erupt.

Nell whined and Harlow couldn't help but feel guilty. "Sorry, girl. You'll be fine here. I'll be right back. I don't know how long I'm going to be in Yellowstone, so I'd really like to watch Old Faithful up close." While she had the chance.

Harlow hurried out of the lodge and started for the geyser when a text came through on her cell. She walked around to the far side of the geyser and hung back near the edge of the boardwalk and the tree line, while reading the text.

Tyson Wilkes, who headed up the RMKU, liked to keep her informed of the unit's comings and goings, and right now, since she was away from their Denver headquarters, she needed the connection. She missed the new friends she'd made when she joined the Rocky Mountain K-9 Unit after leaving her position as a police officer in Santa Fe. The experience had been worth it and she hoped the RMKU would continue to be contracted with the FBI.

She smiled at the text from Tyson. Talk about a cohesive team, the K-9 handlers worked well together. Tyson had hand-picked each one of them from law enforcement agencies across the Rocky Mountain region. He was supportive and encouraging and seemed to have a keen sense when she needed to hear from him.

Like now. She smiled at the texts that came through. Rebel—one of the trainee dogs—had been assigned a handler and was beginning official training as a protection K-9. And the same could hold true for Chase, but Shiloh still struggled.

Harlow texted back.

Glad to hear about the progress. Shiloh will get there!

Tyson replied.

How's your progress going on the task force?

Harlow wasn't sure how much to tell him. They were friends…to a point. So how honest could she be with the unit leader about her past with Wes? Though, really, they were working together fine. Even bringing it up could give Tyson a different idea when things were going well. A few hiccups at the beginning, but today— after the morning meeting—had worked out fine.

The gathering around Old Faithful seemed to tense up at once, expectant. That meant that at any moment now the geyser would spew hot water. She didn't want to miss that.

As well as can be expected. I need to go now but I'll give you more information later.

Pain ignited when strong hands gripped her from behind.

A scream erupted from her throat.

He covered her mouth and tried to slip something over her head as he dragged her deeper into the woods.

Her heart jumped into her throat. Adrenaline spiked. She needed evasive, defensive moves like a head butt. She threw her head back to strike the guy in the nose. He grunted in pain as his hand slipped from her mouth and he lost his grip on her arms. She reached for her gun but he'd already disarmed her, and tossed it to the ground.

She tried to scramble away. "Help! Someone help!"

Harlow turned to run—he was too big to fight, and she no longer had her weapon. But he caught her, covered her mouth again, and dragged her into the woods by her hair.

Wes had just walked away from Ricky in search of Harlow. He'd seen her out by the geyser. A scream rent the air at the same time Old Faith erupted. Wes froze. Had he imagined the sound? No one else seemed to react. In that case, he'd been the only one to hear it.

Harlow...where was she? Panic tried to engulf him as he raced toward the boardwalk where tourists were mesmerized by the hot water spraying high into the air, roaring and bringing the pungent smell of minerals with it. Only a few heads turned and looked as if they'd heard something too.

He wasn't alone, but he was the only one to respond, recognizing the sound.

Heart pounding, he searched for Harlow as well as the source of the scream. *Lord, let it not be another abduction. Let it not be... Harlow...*

Crossing the grass, pine needles, weaving between trees until he was at the wide space surrounding the hydrothermal attraction, he ran along the boardwalk created to protect people from falling into the boiling pools.

Wes searched the woods. "Harlow!" Desperation flooded him. Had she gone back to the lodge and he'd somehow missed it? He held on to that hope but in the meantime, he still had to find the source of that scream.

He hadn't heard it again and doubt began to creep in. Maybe someone had been having fun, and the shriek was part of that. No. That scream had been terror-filled. He recognized it...

Harlow. He knew her voice. That had come from Harlow. *No, Lord. It can't be Harlow. Please let it not be her.*

He knew in his heart that it was. His legs started to shake but he pushed past the panic that would leave him impotent and let determination fuel him instead.

Between the trees, he spotted two people in the woods—struggling. There. Then gone again as they disappeared behind the trees into the ever-darkening forest.

I'm coming, Harlow! Just hold on!
Lord, keep her safe...

He rushed into woods, weaving between the thick pines, in the direction he'd last seen them. The trees grew thicker, the forest darker, as branches reached out as if to hold him back. But nothing would keep him from getting to Harlow.

The sounds were muffled—a woman fighting, a man overpowering her and dragging her through the woods. Sticks cracked; grunts resounded. He raced toward the sounds of an abduction in progress.

Finally he saw them as he rounded a boulder.

A man wearing all black held a knife to Harlow. The man jerked his face up. Though his identity remained in the shadows beneath his hoodie, his reaction told Wes he'd seen him. But Wes was still too far away. The man could disappear again if he didn't catch up. His legs burned as he raced toward them, watching the ground so he wouldn't stumble, but never letting Harlow out of his sight.

What if the man killed her before Wes could get to her? He ignored the thought. No time to let it crush him, paralyze him. Adrenaline drove him forward.

Close enough, he whipped his gun out and aimed. "Let her go."

The man released Harlow—she'd been putting up a fight of her own—and dashed away, disappearing into the trees. Wes wanted to chase him, but Harlow gasped as she dropped to the forest floor. Fear nearly consumed him. Had he been too late? The abductor could have already given her a mortal wound. She could be hurt or dying.

His heart pounded erratically as he dropped to his knees next to Harlow. She remained where she'd fallen. Her face was covered with a heavy scarf or rag. Her shoulders bobbed up and down, as though she was sobbing, but no sounds escaped. Compassion filled his heart.

Compassion and relief that he'd found her. But he couldn't be sure…

"Harlow…" Wes tugged off the scarf to see wide terror-filled eyes, and gently gripped her arms. "Are you okay?"

Of course she wasn't okay.

Gratitude surged in her blue eyes as she pressed her face forward into his shoulder.

"I mean did he hurt you, physically? You're not bleeding, are you?" He cradled her in his arms and comforted her quaking form. She sobbed quietly and, deep inside, he sobbed too.

"No. I'm not bleeding." The words she croaked eased his fears but poured fuel on his anger that she'd been taken.

He squeezed his eyes shut and held her tightly, allowing the soothing words welling up inside to escape his lips in soft whispers. He didn't even recognize himself at this moment. And he sure didn't recognize the tough, capable woman in his arms. But a near miss like this—almost being abducted and possibly by the killer they'd been hunting—would shake anyone to their core. Reduce them to a puddle.

And this was the guy's second attempt.

At least they were in each other's arms now. Professionals and yes...friends with a connection from the past, though they wanted to forget the less than memorable parts.

Darkness closed in around them, and a wolf howled. He couldn't even see the stars for the tree canopy. Would her abductor come back and ambush them in this position? He clearly had his sights set on Harlow as his next victim.

"Harlow," he gently whispered again, "I need to get you back to the lodge where it's safe."

Against his shoulder, she nodded then slowly eased away. Wes didn't let her go so easily, though, and continued to hold her. Grip her. Wanted to pull her closer again. Protectiveness spiked through him, even though he knew Harlow wouldn't want that from him. Or at least admit that she wanted it, much less needed it.

But then again, they all needed each other. Law enforcement needed to have each other's backs. That's all he'd done when rescuing her. He ignored the truth sifting through his heart and mind that she was much more to him than simply a member of his task force team, though he would have done the same for any of them.

Assisting her, he was surprised at how quickly she steadied on her own, after what had just happened. Brandishing his weapon, he searched their surroundings as they walked, in case her attacker returned.

Once they were out of the dark woods and close to a disbursing geyser-watching crowd, he tucked his gun in his shoulder holster and got on his cell. He'd been too focused on getting to her before it was too late, and hadn't yet made the call.

He called Ricky and asked him to inform the rest of the task force, including the sheriff, park law enforcement and rangers, that there was a dangerous man in the woods. An attacker who could be the killer. The woods near Old Faithful needed to be searched and visitors put on alert. He needed to get Harlow someplace safe.

Where was Nell? He glanced around. Panic ensued.

"Where's Nell?" The K-9 hadn't been taken out by Harlow's attacker, had she? The dog would have alerted or possibly defended her in the attack.

"I left her in my room while I watched the eruption."

He chuckled to bring levity. "I've never seen you without Nell. I'm relieved that she wasn't hurt in the attack but…" He stepped back and gave her a closer look. Her holster was empty. "Don't tell me you left your gun in your room too, did you?"

She shook her head, her expression somber. Anger surged in her gaze. "He got the advantage. Disarmed me and tossed it." She vehemently shook her head as she tried to hold herself together in front of him, the task force leader. But he was so much more than that.

"It's okay. Relax. His fingerprints could be on the gun."

"No. He was wearing gloves. Like last time."

"But we could still find DNA on your clothes. I know that didn't work last time, but we should try everything. Even the slightest chance."

She nodded. "I'll change and put them in an evidence bag."

"Fortunately for us, our evidence tech is staying in the lodge." Wes glanced across the dimly lit space around the geyser as they walked. Three task force members rushed forward. "And they're on their way now. The team knows what happened."

And they would have a lot of questions. Was it the same guy as last time? Had the attacker targeted Harlow because of her appearance? Was the man in the black hoodie the same man who'd killed at least one woman and abducted the others who remained missing and were also presumed dead?

Tonight had been a close call. Much too close to death, and Wes struggled to remain composed as Bill, Perry Heigl and Ricky Shore stopped in front of them.

Harlow stood tall and gave her statement to Perry, as did Wes. Bill advised he would need her clothes for possible DNA, then Perry and Ricky took off to search the woods and retrieve her gun to process for possible fingerprints and provide a loaner to her until her gun was returned.

Bill, Harlow and Wes headed for the lodge. Instinctively, he pulled her closer and remained watchful of their surroundings as he ushered her into the lodge and right up the staircase to her door. Inside the room, Nell barked. Bill, having detoured to his room, approached, holding an evidence bag in which she could put her clothing.

Harlow searched her pockets for the keycard.

Wes feared she might have lost it in her struggle with the attacker, but she found it. Her hands trembled and couldn't get it to work.

"Let me try." He took it from her, held it just right and opened the door.

He moved into the room first, to make sure the small space was safe and held no threats, then left her to change.

He waited out in the hallway with Bill. Neither of them spoke, but he suspected the evidence tech struggled to process the same emotions and the incredulity. One of the task force members had almost been abducted—twice. Did the attacker know who she was? Or was it simply her coloring that had drawn his attention?

The door opened and Harlow handed off the evidence bag to Bill.

"I have someone arriving tonight to deliver it to be processed," Bill said. "If there's DNA here, we'll find it and use it to nail this guy."

Harlow shook her head but didn't meet Bill's eyes with her own red-rimmed ones.

Fury boiled through Wes. He couldn't wait to get his hands on the man who'd attacked her, and likely the same man who had already killed Emery and the other missing women. Given how long the other three women had been missing, there was little hope of finding them alive. But Cassidy could still be.

And Harlow was right here.

"I'll talk to you later, Bill." Wes dismissed the man with his words.

Bill nodded and headed down the hall.

Harlow moved to shut her door, but Wes stepped into the room with her before she could close it and then shut it behind him.

"What…what are you doing?" Her striking eyes filled with a mix of pain, relief and terror.

Protection surged in him again, but instead of reaching for her like he wanted to, he remained by the door. What was he doing? Was he afraid to say anything because of what she would think?

"I'm worried about you. Are you sure you're not hurt physically? We could get you to the hospital, or the nearest park clinic."

"I'm a little bruised, yes. I'll be fine, so you can go now."

But she wasn't fine.

Like him, she could be thinking that if he hadn't showed up, she could have been taken away, despite her training in self-defense. This time, the guy had taken her gun and she hadn't happened to have a lug wrench in her hand to bash him with. Then again, Wes held on to the hope that she would have escaped regardless, without his help.

She slowly shook her head and drew in a long inhale. "I didn't thank you. I should have thanked you." She held his gaze. "Thank you for helping me."

Wes couldn't stand the pain in her eyes. The fear. He shouldn't—he really shouldn't—but the circumstances, this situation, called for compassion and reassurance. He wasn't completely sure he wasn't the one who needed that reassurance.

He took a step forward and reached for her. "Come here."

Would she step into his arms so willingly after everything they'd been through?

FIVE

Harlow soaked up the tenderness. She couldn't remember him being this gentle and concerned. But then, she'd never been physically attacked when they were in the academy, and maybe Wes had never had the opportunity to reveal this side of himself.

Sure, they'd had tender moments. Or maybe this was just all her perception, and she was being overemotional. All the law enforcement training she'd received, and all the experience under her belt, had not prepared her for being physically attacked and overcome.

But she was grateful to be alive, and that, thanks to Wes. He'd heard her scream, her cry for help, when no one else had. And she would never forget that he'd saved her life. And somehow it transformed how she felt about him.

Into what, she didn't know.

Rivals. Friends. Romantic interests. Whatever they were before, they were something different now, and she couldn't figure it out. All she knew was that she could stay in his arms forever...except that wasn't reality. No. Reality was what had happened tonight. A shudder ran through her, and the feel of the assailant's grip on her arms flashed through her mind. She was going to lose it in front of Wes, and she couldn't afford that.

Digging deep into her soul, she found the strength she needed, took a slow, calming breath, and stepped out of his arms. He'd become...too personal.

"Harlow... It's just me. It's okay..."

She searched his eyes. "You're right. It's okay. I'm good, Wes."

Putting some much-needed distance between them, she knelt at the crate to release Nell, who wagged her tail as she exited and circled Harlow. Hugging Nell, Harlow ran her fingers through her coarse fur. She needed this momentary small distraction from the reality that she had just been attacked...again.

Wes dropped into the chair in the corner. Maybe he was waiting with her because it was likely someone else might have questions. The sheriff? A park ranger? The cold reality seeped in and a shiver ran over her. They would all want to know if she thought it could be the same guy. She couldn't be one hundred percent sure, but the physicality matched.

Nell whined, obviously sensing Harlow's distress.

"Can I get you anything?" Wes asked, concern and something more she couldn't define filling his tone.

Harlow kept her head down and almost buried it in the beagle's fur. She shook her head, unable to trust her voice just yet.

"Harlow." Wes stood from the chair and paced.

She looked up.

"I'm staying in that chair tonight while you get some rest. You don't have your weapon."

The news shocked her. She didn't want or need him in the room with her.

Brutal hands gripped her arms, tugged her backward. Covered her mouth...

She had to work hard to keep her composure. "Wes, I'm fine, really, there's no need."

He opened the minifridge, tugged out a bottle of water and handed it to her. "Oh, there's a need all right. Maybe I need it. Maybe I'm the one who needs to know that you're okay."

And she saw it then. The pain and the fear in his eyes. If Wes was that worried...

She took the bottle and then rose to sit on the edge of the bed. Harlow took a long drink while she measured her next words. She needed to tell him the truth. It would be worse if he found out later and that she hadn't told him.

She hung her head.

"Are you sure you don't need a doctor? Your superior is going to insist you see a therapist, of course. This guy is *after* you, Harlow."

Tyson. Oh no. She snapped her eyes back up. "What? No. I'm fine. Really. Just stunned, Wes."

"No less than I am. Are you…are you okay to talk about it?"

A small laugh escaped. His tenderness could undo her. This was big, bad Wes Grey, after all.

"What's so funny?"

You. "Nothing. Yes, I'm fine to talk."

"What were you doing out there, really?"

Um…she'd been trying to avoid him when she'd left the lodge and headed to the geyser. Go figure. But she wouldn't tell him that. "Really. I wanted to see the geyser. I'm glad you were there to… Thanks for saving me from him. A possible serial killer."

"I'm just glad I was there. But I have no doubt that you would have gotten free."

Yeah. Right. She had already tried. But she wouldn't have stopped trying, so maybe he was right. If only she'd been holding a lug wrench or, at the very least, she'd had her gun in her grip. She wanted to thank him for his kindness, but it seemed awkward. She hugged herself.

Wes stood and moved to grab the extra quilt and place it over her shoulders.

He was going over and above—wasn't he? Was she imagining it? She had no choice but to tell him; she couldn't keep the truth from him. It would hurt her too much, and probably him too.

"I need to tell you something."

He sat in the chair again and the way he looked at her, his eyes seemed to search her soul as if it were completely laid bare for his perusal.

"I'm listening."

Oh yeah, he was listening. Of that, she had no doubt. "This isn't easy for me."

"Whatever it is, you can trust me. You can tell me."

Could she really trust him, especially when he had no idea what she would share? Probably not. "About the attack tonight."

It was her turn to search *his* soul. What was he thinking? He appeared to want to say something, and she would let him. That might help steer the conversation.

He was waiting. Patiently.

"I thought about not calling in the first incident," she said. "When he grabbed me while I changed the tire."

Wes sat up then, his eyes practically spearing through her heart. "What? Why?" She didn't answer right away.

He scraped a hand through his thick hair. "Why would you even consider keeping that to yourself?"

He stood and she did, too, needing to maintain control instead of losing it. She kept her voice low and her tone even. "Because I was afraid I'd be cut from the team for my own protection."

He studied her as if measuring her words. Or perhaps measuring his response.

She'd known Wes a long time and knew that he was always composed. That he'd lost it so easily just now told her volumes—that he still had feelings for her. Feelings he probably didn't want.

And she didn't want that from him either.

Did she?

He paced the small space, appeared to compose himself, then eased into the seat once again. "Okay, this is me not overreacting. I'm glad you got away from him that first time on your own. I know you're capable. And I believe you would have earlier, too—even if I hadn't found you."

She was so relieved, she couldn't speak. But now things were different. Now, she was clearly more than just a blue-eyed blonde in her twenties. Now, she was a real target.

"I want to hear everything again, Harlow. Give me the details. Did you see his face at all? Any part?"

"No. He approached from behind and tried to drag me away. I don't think he tried to put something over my face. Maybe he just hadn't gotten to that point yet."

"And you swung the lug wrench over your head and it connected."

She nodded. "He ran away in pain. He wasn't wearing black, but he was in a hoodie and jeans. Looked like any other park visitor. It's why the rangers and the local police couldn't find him. He didn't look suspicious in the slightest."

"So our perp happens upon you, a woman with blond hair and blue eyes, and made his move. You escaped, and maybe that, coupled with the fact you injured him, makes you even more of a target. He somehow followed you, or has been searching for you, starting with the Old Faithful district. And now he's found you."

She brought her knees up and wrapped her arms around them, tucking her chin down. She didn't look like a professional at the moment, but she'd gone from fitting the profile of the victims to becoming an actual target—twice.

His gray eyes had turned dark, hurt and anger sparking in them. "I can't believe you considered not calling it in."

"Don't look at me like that. I need to prove that Nell and I can do the job."

"And you have."

She sensed a "but" in there. "Then don't punish me, take this opportunity away from me, because I'm a target and he's clearly after *me* now—not just because of my resemblance."

Wes said nothing for a long time. He stared at Nell, but Harlow could tell that he was deep in thought. She wished he would share what he was thinking. Her insides roiled. Would he send her packing back to Denver now?

God, please no. It isn't fair.

She couldn't take it anymore. "Please let me stay on the task force." *For old times' sake. I've earned it.* She wouldn't say the words, because then she would be downright begging. Okay, maybe she would if she had to.

Harlow couldn't breathe.

"As I mentioned, you're a valuable member of the team. Replacing you would take time we don't have."

Oddly, the fact that he was thinking in professional terms kind of hurt, but she held on to hope. "What are you saying? I can stay?"

"You're in danger, Harlow. We both know that. I hope I'm not making a mistake here, but you can stay…under one condition."

"And what's that?" She had a feeling she wasn't going to like the condition.

"You stick with me at all times. With

a kidnapper and possible serial killer out there, none of us should be working alone, especially not you, since you're a target. So no more wandering off to take Nell on a walk or by yourself like you did tonight. Do you agree?"

Her throat constricted and she couldn't swallow. She had plenty to say in response, but those words were far from her agreement. In the end, Wes had the advantage—if she pushed it, then she could hightail it back to Denver. She would be off the FBI task force.

And if she chose to stay in this, then there would be no escaping Wes Grey.

"Agreed."

Wes sat in the chair comfortable enough one could fall asleep—if one were exhausted. Except in his case, he might be exhausted but his mind wouldn't shut down to the reality that Harlow had almost been taken again.

Almost…murdered.

He hadn't wanted to even think the thought, much less speak it. But it remained lodged in his gut. He replayed the events a thousand times in his head. He'd seen her out there—but with Nell. If he'd seen her alone, would he have gone to check on her before she'd needed his help? When, in truth, he'd escaped dinner as fast as he could, needing fresh air that wasn't filled with her vanilla scent.

And see what had happened? He couldn't let her out of his sight until this was over. He'd counted the logs on all the walls in the room, and trusses on the ceiling…anything to keep from looking at her sleeping form. He suspected she wouldn't be able to sleep, and she'd tossed and turned for hours. Maybe sleep was impossible for them both, but he wasn't leaving.

That madman was still out there, and Wes was sure she was being specifically targeted now. Did the guy know where she was? He pressed his palm over his gun, which rested on the table next to him, and squeezed the grip. Somehow it felt reassuring. His laptop was open on his lap so he could write reports, respond to emails, and research.

With a pillow tucked under her head, he noted that Harlow had finally settled into a position facing the wall.

The chair might be comfortable for one night, but it would be uncomfortable for two. He couldn't leave her to go to his own room, but this setup wasn't sustainable for the remainder of this investigation. Still, it would work for now. He'd known he wouldn't be able to sleep tonight anyway, so guarding her in her room had seemed like the only option.

If the attacker had found her in the Old Faithful district, he could very well locate her at the lodge. For those task force members who required it, Wes would find other accommodations for the rest of their stay, but especially for Harlow and him. A place where he could keep an eye out for her... in more spacious quarters.

Was he nuts to consider this? He'd hated the anxiety in her eyes over the possibility she would be taken off the investigation. But despite her greatest fear that she would be removed from the task force, she'd done the right thing and called in that first attack because it was good police protocol and important for the safety of the park. She was a professional through and through.

And so much more.

He rubbed his temples and tried not to look at her soft blond hair spilling over her pillow, or her sleeping form.

The thing was, even if he wanted to send her back to Denver and replace her with another K-9 handler, then he would just have to worry about her in Denver or wherever else she might be assigned. Her two-time attacker—if he was the serial killer—could just follow her there.

So he'd trust her to continue to do her job here.

Being with her now, working this real

investigation as opposed to an academy training exercise, reminded him of the reason he'd been drawn to her in the first place eight years ago.

He couldn't so easily forget the past, when it came to those good memories, though he should. He really should. If he didn't, he might find himself being drawn to her again. She was beautiful and strong and brilliant. Intensely focused on her job. And so was he.

So like before, in the end, Wes was no good at relationships. With no significant other in her life, it would seem she wasn't either.

He and Harlow together in that sense would never work.

Remember that.

Because what was he doing even thinking about that at a time like this? He glanced around the small space he was sharing with Harlow. If there was another way, he wouldn't be here.

But her life was at risk.

He wanted to stand and pace the room, but he would wake her—if she were really sleeping. Instead, he crept across the room, snuck through the door and leaned against the wall in the corridor. There. Better. He could breathe now.

And with the space came the clarity. Wes realized the real reason his thoughts had focused on protecting Harlow and what he'd had with her before—but she had almost been taken today. He could never let that happen. He would admit that it might be better if someone else on the task force guarded her, but he trusted no one else with her life.

I can do this...

He definitely needed to get some sleep—or at least a big black pot of strong coffee—if he was going to find a killer.

Outside her room, he could see across the expanse of the lobby and he stared at the mounted heads of wildlife—moose, buffalo, elk and more. The sight churned his insides as it reminded him of the hunter and the prey.

And Harlow... He'd almost chuckle to himself if it wasn't so serious—he could see her considering using herself as bait. Then again that would be more like something he might have done years ago—pushing the envelope to get the job done. Harlow, on the other hand, was all about following the rules, so he could breathe easy that she would never try something so daring.

The door opened, startling him, and Harlow stuck her head out, her tousled hair hanging to the side when she angled toward him. Concern shifted into a smile, then heat warmed her cheeks.

Beautiful.

"Did you sleep out here?" Her voice held a teasing tone.

"Not while I'm watching out for you." He stifled a yawn.

"Give me a second to change, and then

you can go with me to take Nell for a walk."

"Then let's get some strong coffee and breakfast." He returned her smile, appreciating that she was adhering to their agreement. "We can talk about the investigation."

She closed the door. He wasn't on security duty and he wasn't sure he could keep this up, but somehow he had to find a way.

A few moments later, she emerged from the room dressed in cargo pants and a thick hoodie over a T-shirt, her blond hair tucked into the hood. She secured Nell's leash, then blinked up at Wes, her blue eyes bright. Wow. She looked entirely more refreshed than he would have expected.

Except, fear lingered in her gaze.

Good. A healthy dose of fear would help keep her safe.

SIX

After breakfast and a brief confab with task force members, Harlow secured Nell in the back of Wes's SUV and he steered them away from the Old Faithful attraction. She appreciated that he didn't subject her to a lot of questions—most of the members had dialed in over a video chat conferencing app.

While he drove, she stared out the window at the mountains, the forest and the steam rising up here and there, marking a hydrothermal pool or geyser. But she wasn't interested in those—she wanted to spot the guy in the hoodie. And this time, she'd try to catch more details about him. His jawline, hard or fleshy? His scent. Any visible scars. As far as she was concerned, every guy in a hoodie was the guy who attacked her. Of course, that wasn't true, but until she knew differently, she would treat each person as a potential killer. It made sense that the guy who'd grabbed her last night was the man they were after.

Wes turned out of the park and sped up, the trees whipping by. The thick forest reminded her of how much she loved exploring the woods near Santa Fe where she'd grown up, stepping on the pine needles, breathing in the scent of pine and juniper. Then, after moving, exploring the fresh territory with Nell in the mountains near Denver and, just two days ago, she'd come to Yellowstone National Park in Wyoming.

Grief twisted inside—after two near abductions in the woods, she struggled to keep the fear from stealing her joy over the beauty of God's creation. This kind of wariness was a new experience for her. It made her suspicious of every shadow and wondering who was lurking behind every tree.

She didn't like it. Not one bit. She'd just have to overcome it.

"You okay?" Wes asked.

"Of course, why do you ask?" He was much too perceptive, or maybe a little too concerned. But she appreciated it. He was a task force leader who cared about those he worked with.

His cell phone buzzed, and he steered onto the shoulder to respond to a text. While they sat next to the road, she kept watching the woods. She hoped they caught the killer before he moved on from Yellowstone.

Finished with his text, Wes set his cell on the console and sighed. His hand rested on the gearshift, but he didn't move it to steer them back onto the road.

Uh-oh. What now? "What's going on?"

"I got the intel for the campsites for two of the guys Cassidy Leidel wrote up—

Harrison Cahn and Martin Barnes—as well as some background on them."

"That's good, isn't it? But then something's bothering you."

"I've been thinking about this all morning, and I can't put it to rest."

Harlow didn't press him but waited instead for him to continue.

He swiveled toward her. She wasn't prepared for the intensity in his gaze, though she should have been.

"If our killer is behind Cassidy's disappearance," he said, "I have to wonder why he hasn't moved on to the next place instead of hanging around. His past MO is to abduct his victim and then set off for the next park. Emery's body was found— which is why those working the case believe the other victims are dead rather than hidden away. Instead, he's remained and tried to take you—twice. Add to that, he knows law enforcement is crawling over Yellowstone, looking for him. Visitors are on alert as well, and many are heading home early with the news of a possible threat out there."

Harlow pursed her lips. Hadn't she just been thinking along those same lines? "Does that mean that you're scrapping the plan to interview Harrison and Martin. You think it's a waste of time?"

"No. But, honestly, I don't know what to think." He dipped his chin, his gray eyes measuring her. "If our man is staying around, I can't help but think it has everything to do with..." His words trailed off and a pained expression crossed his face.

She understood. He couldn't finish the words. But she would finish for him. "Me. I got away on that first day. He can't stand the idea that I won, so he tried again." She sank lower in the seat. "And I got away a second time, only because you showed up." *With your gun.*

She fisted her hands, wishing she'd not lost her weapon. Wes had been authorized to provide her a loaner until her department-issued gun was returned. The evidence team had found her gun in the woods and kept it. She pressed her hand over the borrowed gun in her holster.

God, is that it? Is that why he's still here? Am I making a mistake by insisting I stay?

Wes pressed his hand over hers. "We agreed you would stick close to me. I've informed the others—discreetly—so you wouldn't feel uncomfortable. But we've got your back, Harlow."

"Maybe I was wrong to insist on staying on the task force."

"It's your call, of course. I haven't been completely honest with you, though." He squeezed her hand and then released it. She shifted to look at him as he hung his head.

Her heart pounded. What would he say? "I'm listening."

"Even if I tried to send you back to Denver for your own safety, Harlow, I'm concerned this guy just might follow you there. He jumps around from park to park, looking for his next victim. If he's obsessed with you, what's to keep him from going to Denver?"

Good point. "You think I'm safer here with you."

He lifted his head and stared into the woods, obvious distress carving lines she hadn't seen eight years ago around his eyes, across his forehead and mouth. "I might be wrong. My judgment might be clouded because of our history together. But I wouldn't be able to focus on the investigation if I was worried about you out there alone in Denver, or wherever else you might go, until we have taken down this killer."

Tumultuous emotions swirled around in her mind, entangling with logic and reason. She couldn't find words to respond. Was it that he cared about her that much? Or was he just being a good FBI agent, looking out for someone in danger? She couldn't know which, but some of the wall around her heart crumbled. And, oh, she couldn't fall for this guy again. She couldn't let herself be hurt again.

But she could definitely stay here with him and take him up on the additional protection—that is, until the killer was caught. She glanced out the window and shivered a bit. "I'm glad this guy we're after doesn't have one of those names the media gives out. Like 'Parks Killer.' Especially because he's after *me*."

He nodded. "I don't like the idea of naming him, giving him any kind of notoriety. Let's stop him before he kills one more person so the media won't have a chance to give him a name, because he doesn't deserve one. He doesn't have serial killer status until we find another body."

That didn't mean he wasn't a serial killer, just that they couldn't confirm it yet. But she had a feeling they all knew that this guy had killed all the women who had been abducted. Hence…

"I've done some basic research on serial killers and have read all the FBI profiler reports that my boss's assistant texted me when I was en route here, but I don't know as much as I should. And I think that even if we confirm he is a serial killer, he doesn't deserve a name. Maybe killers like him are looking to get attention. We're not going to give it to him beyond taking him down."

"I like your attitude." His face relaxed, as if tension eased out of it at her words, and he shifted into gear. "Let's find Harrison's campground and on the way there, I'll educate you on serial killers—the quick-start course."

Good. She didn't like sitting next to the road, especially since it edged the forest— in case the killer had somehow tracked and followed them and was lurking behind the trees.

"We've already talked about how they usually target victims with similar demographics or appearances, and that has certainly turned out to be true in this case."

A shudder crawled over her. "I should

dye my hair and wear contacts to change my eye color."

Wes had stopped at an intersection and, at her words, turned to look at her. His eyes roamed her hair and face. The way he looked at her caused her belly to thrum. She was relieved when he turned his attention back to the road and made a right.

"What else can you tell me?" she asked.

"There are so many nuances and too many details, but I can tell you that they suffer from varying degrees of mental illness, are often victims of abuse, and perpetrators of petty crimes. Not every instance is the same, but they often have trouble staying employed."

"Do we know anything on Harrison's and Martin's backgrounds?"

"I have people digging into that."

"So we're going to question them solely on the fact that they had encounters with Cassidy this last week."

"That, and Harrison was a handyman in New Mexico."

She gasped at the news. New Mexico. "Where the first abduction occurred." Her breathing quickened. "And Martin?"

"An unemployed janitor from Utah."

Where the third victim had disappeared. This was the intel he'd mentioned earlier. Either of them could be the killer. "And you already dismissed David Ellison?"

"Yes and no. He's a local, but he has a history of violence, and Cassidy was working with him to try to rehabilitate him. I don't like him for this, but we'll question him all the same. Maybe she had been working with the others too. He could have killed her...as a copycat, even. Or her death isn't related to the killer. All questions we have to answer."

Harlow nodded, taking it all in. "The point is that they all three had encounters with her and knew her."

"And unfortunately, all three are looking good in terms of fitting the description of a serial killer."

When Harlow met each man, would she

be able to tell if one of them had been the man to grab her from behind? Or would *he* react to seeing her?

As much as they needed to catch this guy, the thought of facing him over the next few hours made her skin crawl. But she'd rather do this—on her terms—than on the terms of a killer—serial or not.

Wes cracked his window as he drove.

And listened.

His erratic pulse was an unfortunate distraction as he slowly steered through the campground where the killer could be staying. He could be bringing Harlow right to the man's door, so he remained vigilant, alert to every shadow, every sound. The grounds were clean and tidy, free of garbage and food that could attract bears.

He was attuned to the subtle shift in Harlow's demeanor, though it was likely she didn't want him to know—but she was scared. And by keeping her here with him on the task force, he was putting her through a kind of nightmare despite what she'd said about wanting to stay. Still, she hid it well, putting on a strong front, and he trusted her to remain equally vigilant and on guard, bringing her skills and professional experience with her to meet a potential serial killer. The man was here in the park somewhere.

Maybe at this campground.

Wes backed the SUV up into an empty campsite.

"What are you doing?"

"I want to get the lay of the land." Before driving into the campground, he'd stopped at the office and grabbed a map, which he now opened. "I was told that Harrison is camping at site number 84. Loops C-84."

"That's across two loops and three campsites over."

"Yes. And a vehicle is parked there." Wes folded the map. "Listen, you could stay here in the SUV while I talk to him, if you'd prefer. Lock the doors and honk if there's trouble, but I doubt anyone is going to bother you. I'll be close."

"What is the point of me being here at all if you aren't going to use Nell? Wes… listen to me." Her voice nearly shook with frustration. "If there's the scent of death on either of these guys or their gear, then Nell could pick that up. You need me to go with you. Don't waste the resources given to you."

She was right and he knew it. He'd always been so decisive, even when crossing lines to get things done.

But now…he kept wavering in his decision to keep her here.

Wes sat taller and rubbed his jaw. He wasn't thinking clearly and needed to shrug off the ridiculous emotion clouding his judgment. He needed to maintain his own skill and professionalism and to stop worrying so much about Harlow. She would be fine as long as she didn't go into the woods alone. Or *anywhere*…alone, really.

"Right. You're right."

She blew out a slow, even breath. Maybe thought he hadn't noticed her relief. "Even though we're dressed to fit in around the park, and Nell isn't wearing her vest as we search the campground, a dog sniffing around could still make him nervous, especially after we identify ourselves. That is, if he has committed a crime."

"If he runs, then we'll know why, and we'll give chase and capture him." Wes was glad he sounded more confident than he felt. "All right. Let's do this."

He shared a quick look with her.

He and Harlow, working together. He never would have dreamed this scenario up in a million years.

He opened the door and moved to the back of the vehicle with Harlow to secure Nell. They'd both dressed in camping attire—cargo pants, hoodies and sneakers—to fit in. Harlow had started wearing her hair down—long and wavy—instead of in the usual ponytail. Was that to draw the killer in?

His heart hammered. Maybe that wasn't such a good idea. Still, her hair was silky and beautiful, and he remembered weaving his fingers through it—years ago. Wes glanced across the campsites at their destination and focused his thoughts.

Together they strolled with Nell, looking like they were a couple walking their dog. He thought to hold her hand and add to their happy-couple appearance, but they weren't here undercover. Then again, he *wanted* to hold her hand.

Wrong time. Wrong place.

Never going to happen.

As they neared a blue nylon tent, larger than a pup tent, he focused on the road and on Nell, while at the same time taking in site C-84. Harrison had exited the tent and was building a fire. He slowly stood, as if his skin had prickled with their presence, and turned around.

Uncanny.

His fortysomething face looked rough with its graying stubble. The man showed no emotion at all. His brown eyes were stone cold. Serial killer or not, this guy wasn't normal. Normal would have meant curiosity springing into his eyes, or a smile. Something. Instead, a wall had gone right up.

"Can I help you?" he asked.

This could be the moment that Harrison would run. Wes braced himself for that possibility, if this guy was their killer. Or he could be guilty of other crimes.

Wes sensed he was guilty of something. He tugged his credentials out. "I'm FBI Special Agent Wes Grey, and I'd like to ask you a few questions." He purposely didn't introduce Harlow. If Harrison *didn't* know her name, didn't know her beyond the fact that she was the blue-eyed blonde who'd gotten away from him twice—he wasn't going to give it to him.

The man stiffened and his eyes shot to the dog.

Oh, so he *could* react, and wasn't totally in control of his emotions. Wes watched for recognition in the man's eyes—if he was after Harlow, could Wes read that in his expression?

Wes nodded to Harlow, signaling her to give the command.

"Ready to work Nell?' The beagle wagged her tail.

"Find Trudy." She gave the command she'd created specifically for Nell—nothing too gruesome or too general—but kept the dog on a leash.

The dog instantly started sniffing around the tent and Harlow gave her plenty of space to do it, following her.

"Hey, what are you doing?" Harrison fisted his hands.

Time for Wes to redirect. "How long have you been here in Yellowstone?"

Harrison narrowed his gaze on Nell and Harlow, then slowly looked at Wes. "A couple of weeks, man. What's this about?"

"Where were you before you came here?"

"I'm from New Mexico." His cold eyes

kept darting to Nell, but he never once looked at Harlow. Did he purposefully avoid looking at a woman he targeted, fearing Wes would see the truth in his eyes? Or was he more concerned that Nell would find something he didn't want found?

"What did you do in New Mexico?"

"Look. I got nothing to hide. So I'm not going to tell you to go get a warrant. I watch TV. I know that you'll think I done something wrong. I was a handyman there. I'm a handyman here. I've been looking for a permanent home and job. That's not against the law."

True enough. "Have you made any friends here, specifically with park rangers?"

"Sure. I know the guy up at the park office."

"Anyone else? Say…any females?"

Harrison eased into a camping chair. "I know Cassidy Leidel. She was helping me."

He hung his head. Guilt finally getting to him?

"When was the last time you saw her?"

The guy lifted his head and those stone-cold eyes suddenly shed emotion—regret and sadness. "I know she's missing. She was going to help me look at some work around here as a handyman. She was going to recommend me. You think I would harm someone who wanted to help me?"

No. Probably not. With the man's reaction, Wes had a hard time believing Harrison was their guy, though killers could fool people. "Is there anything you know about her or could tell us that would help us find out what happened to her?"

Harrison scraped a hand across his ruddy, stubbled jaw. "If I did, if I knew what happened, if someone hurt her, then I would have come to you first. That is, after I found the man who hurt her."

Harrison sounded emotionally attached to Cassidy. Protective. A man smitten, maybe? Harlow returned with Nell by her side and subtly shook her head.

"Would you allow the dog to sniff around inside your tent and your vehicle?" If Harrison gave permission, then Wes wouldn't need a warrant and, at the moment, he had no probable cause to get one.

Harrison lifted his hands in surrender, appearing nothing like the man they had approached moments before. "Go ahead and look around."

Still, the man's eyes watched Nell. He was afraid of something. Definitely afraid Nell would find whatever he was hiding.

"Nell is a cadaver dog, Harrison," Wes said as Harlow and the beagle went inside. "If you haven't killed anyone, you have nothing to fear."

"Right. Now that the feds are searching my camp with a dog, the neighbors will be suspicious of me. I'm going to have to move, man."

Harlow returned from the tent with Nell again, shaking her head. Next, she searched the inside of his Ford truck, which was in his view, and came up empty.

Wes had hoped to end their search today. Harrison was only one of the men on his radar though. "Thanks for your cooperation. If you see anything or hear anything that could help us in our search for Cassidy, please call me." Wes handed his card to the man.

Harrison's hand shook as he took it and pocketed it.

Wes and Harlow turned their backs on him and exited the campsite, then headed up the road. Harlow was about to turn toward the SUV but stopped.

"Let's let Nell search along the drive as we make our way around the camp," she said. "The guy who attacked me has to be camping nearby somewhere, though maybe it's a completely different campground altogether."

He nodded. "We'll get to Martin Barnes afterward."

Harlow gave Nell the search command again, then walked next to him. Harlow's demeanor understandably more relaxed than when they'd approached. "What did you think of Harrison?"

"I think he's guilty of something."

She let out Nell's leash a bit more, allowing the beagle to sniff the perimeter of the tree line. "Of what?"

"Not abduction and murder, necessarily, but he was nervous. So I think he's guilty of something. He was afraid Nell was going to find something."

"Drugs?"

"Possibly. We can let the rangers and the sheriff know about what happened, and they can keep an eye on him. Just because Nell didn't alert, and he seemed genuinely upset about Cassidy's disappearance, doesn't mean he's off the hook."

Harlow nodded. "And in the meantime, we head to the next campground and interview Martin Barnes."

They walked along the other side of the tree line, but Nell didn't alert there either.

Harlow blew out a long breath as, once

they were at the SUV, Wes opened up the back for Nell to get into her crate.

After giving Nell water and a treat, Harlow secured the beagle then stepped back, and when she looked up, her gaze snagged on his face then traveled up to his eyes. He took in her smooth, beautiful skin and those beautiful baby blues. His breath caught in his throat.

Harlow's life was in danger, but Wes would protect her...with his own.

If only he had a clue about how he was going to protect his heart.

SEVEN

Harlow was beyond relieved to finally arrive at their destination so that they could question the potential suspect—Martin Barnes. The drive to the northeast side of the park had taken them far longer than they'd expected. Wes had insisted they stop and grab lunch at Mammoth Springs near the northwest entrance to the park, and then they moved on to Canyon Village, which was quite the drive around to the east side. They'd had to travel in a big circle to get there. Yellowstone, with all its hydrothermal attractions, encompassed a massive caldera that was spread over forty miles or so, with additional hydrothermal activities—like Mammoth—outside the actual caldera.

Miles and miles of driving the two-lane road, slowing down to wait for a herd of buffalo or tourists stopping traffic to catch photographs of a grizzly, could be exhausting.

Wes had parked at the visitors' information center and gone inside and she'd waited inside the locked SUV, watching a couple of campers pull out of the sparsely occupied campground. It was much less crowded this time of year, and frankly, that should make their job easier.

Wes got back in and handed her the map. "This campground will be closing at the end of the month, so Martin will be moving out soon."

"Do you think he would move to another campground in Yellowstone or out of the park completely?"

"The only campground that's open year-round is at Mammoth Springs."

"Mammoth Hot Springs? We were just there today."

"Yes, and we're packing up tonight and moving into a cabin in that district."

"We are? Why?"

"They had an opening. Someone's moving out, so I booked it for us. I think you know why. He found you at Old Faithful and I don't want to risk staying there."

Moving made sense and she wouldn't argue, but she dreaded having to reorient to a whole new place. "What about the rest of the task force? Are they moving too?"

"Those who need to be close have accommodations nearby. Ricky, Tanner and Bill for sure."

"All because I was attacked at Old Faithful." It was a statement, not a question.

"Isn't that reason enough?"

Definitely. Harlow struggled to wrap her mind around everything that had happened since she'd arrived, not the least of which was facing Wes again after so many years and working with him. She had to admit being so close to him for what seemed like 24/7—though they hadn't been together that many days—was wearing on her. Not necessarily in a bad way, but the butterflies in her stomach fluttered at certain looks he gave her. Warmth flooded her belly at other times. And now, in the cab of his truck, the subtle smell of his masculine cologne mixed with a woodsy scent wrapped around her, teasing her.

She shook off the thoughts.

The interior of his SUV felt much too warm, and she had no doubt her proximity to Wes had everything to do with it.

She pulled her hair into a ponytail. "And that leads me to my next question. If Martin Barnes is camping all the way up here, why would he be at Old Faithful stalking *me*? Or around that region at all?"

"That's a great observation, Harlow." Wes shifted the SUV into gear and started the slow drive through the campsites. "Barnes moved to this campground last night. According to the ranger I spoke with, Barnes had been camping closer to Old Faithful at Grant Village. One has to wonder why he would move here only to be moving again since it's going to close. The ranger told me Barnes had already booked this campground two days ago, and that it isn't unusual for tourists to move closer to the hydrothermal features they'd be exploring."

"So, nothing out of the ordinary."

"Not yet." He steered at a crawl through the campground while peering at each of the RVs and tents until he found a vacant site. Then he drove through the small circular drive and stopped.

"Which one is his campsite?"

"D-47. You can see the older fifth-wheel RV just beyond the pup tent across from us. The ranger said he remembered Martin because he'd been looking for work. He directed him to apply online."

"Ah." Harlow nodded. "That figures. It's the only way anymore. What was Martin's reaction to that?"

"The ranger said that he scowled at him."

Harlow sucked in a breath. "Seriously?

Well, that tells us something about the man we're going to question next."

Wes peered through his window.

"The problem we have now is that he's not home. There's no vehicle at the campsite other than the RV." Wes shifted in his seat and grabbed his binoculars.

What more did he think he would see with them?

Both disappointment and relief filled her. She wanted to get it over with and catch their man, but at the same time, if Barnes was the man who'd tried to abduct her, if he was Emery's killer, she dreaded facing him.

"I take it that we're going to wait for him. In the meantime," she added, "we can walk the campground and pretend we belong. Nell will alert us if she finds anything."

Once the beagle was leashed up, Harlow walked along the campground road with Wes. She needed to focus on the task, but her mind worked on multiple issues at the same time, including moving to Mammoth tonight. "You know it'll probably be dark by the time we get back to the Old Faithful district. Do you really think it's a good idea to move tonight?" This wasn't her call, and she should stop trying to control the situation.

"The arrangements have already been made."

Right. His voice sounded strained.

"Okay. But it's a lot of trouble to go to just for me."

What are you doing?

Wes stopped walking, and Harlow pulled Nell back and turned to look at him.

His jaw was working. Oh no. She'd gone too far.

He stared at her for a few heartbeats. Measuring his words? Then he finally said, "I've told you that you're an important part of the task force. The most valuable asset on the team, in my opinion." He leaned in, and she had the distinct sense he wanted to say more. Do more…like cup her cheek. He used to do that on occasion when they were dating.

Memories and emotions flooded her, and she reflexively shut her eyes. Could she be any less professional?

She sucked in a breath and opened them—and noticed a car turning in—a distraction for which she was grateful. "Someone's coming."

He backed away. "Don't look at the car. Just keep walking."

But he reached for her free hand and held it. A spark of energy ran up her arm at his touch. What had been his intentions moments before? She would probably never know, and no way would she ask him. At the moment, he was trying to make them look like a couple, nothing more.

"What kind of vehicle was it?" he asked.

"An older model Chevy truck. A Silverado." Lots of trucks and SUVs around the park, which made sense. People needed to tow their campers and pack camping gear.

"That's Barnes."

"What's the plan?" she asked.

"We'll keep walking slowly around until we come to the campsite."

"Are we going to keep holding hands?" Because that would seem strange for him to then introduce himself as a federal agent.

In answer, he instantly dropped her hand, and she focused on calming her breaths as they approached the RV and the parked Silverado. Barnes hopped out and started pulling firewood out of the back of the truck and placing it near the RV. When he straightened, he turned and saw them. He almost stumbled but smoothly righted himself.

Had she imagined the misstep?

Wes approached Barnes, who retrieved a hydro flask from the picnic table and drank from it, his hand shaking as it gripped the flask.

Barnes finished a long swallow and then turned to Wes. "You're trespassing."

Wes didn't flinch. "Martin Barnes?"

"Who wants to know?"

Tugging his credentials out, Wes flashed them. "I'm FBI Special Agent Wes Grey."

Barnes's eyes briefly flicked to Harlow then down to Nell. Something flashed in his dark gaze—curiosity? Because Wes hadn't introduced her. Or was it something much more ominous. Harlow couldn't say she recognized the man because whoever had attacked her twice now, she hadn't seen. She glanced to his arm—the one she'd hit with the lug wrench. Barnes wore a long-sleeve shirt, so she couldn't see a bruise, nor did he appear injured.

The guy grabbed his flask and plopped into the one folding chair. "I'd offer you a seat, but I'm fresh out. There's the picnic table, of course."

"We're fine." Wes nodded to Harlow.

She took that as his signal to command Nell to sniff around the camp.

"What's with the dog?" Barnes asked, his eyes skewering both Nell and Harlow.

"Nell has special skills." Wes didn't elaborate.

Harlow focused on the K-9 and tried to listen as Wes questioned Martin, asking similar questions that he'd asked Harrison. Then she heard the last question. "Mind if the dog sniffs around in your RV?"

She glanced up in time to see Martin rise from his chair, then open the door and, with a flourish, urge them inside. She gave Nell the command and the beagle bounded up the steps inside the camper. A shiver crawled over Harlow as she passed Martin. Just her imagination or was the guy guilty of abducting blonde, blue-eyed females? Or, as Wes had suggested about Harrison, was Martin guilty of something, if not murder?

Nell sniffed around a pristine interior, and honestly, it wasn't at all what Harlow had expected to see. In the end, the K-9 had detected nothing, which also surprised Harlow.

But she had no business suspecting

every man she saw of Cassidy's disappearance, or the murder of other women, or of trying to abduct her twice. Wes offered his card to Martin and asked him to contact them if he saw anything suspicious.

Once again, Martin drank from the flask, which slightly trembled in his hand. An alcoholic? Or...was he nervous because he was guilty?

On the walk back to the Suburban, they remained quiet. Martin had disappeared inside his RV. While Wes spoke with someone on his cell, Harlow secured Nell in her crate, exhaustion trying to creep in. In all of the cases she had worked with Nell, she had never been asked to accompany an FBI agent to search the premises of prospective serial killers. She closed up the back of his SUV, then turned to find him standing much too close.

Again.

At the disquiet in his gray eyes, she asked, "What's wrong?"

He held both hands near her arms but

didn't connect. She could see clearly that he wanted to, and she wanted that from him as well.

"Are you okay?" he asked.

Wow. She was better before he seemed to care about her so much, and she wanted to curl into that concern and protective-ness. To feel safe. But that would be a bad idea. A *very* bad idea. She was losing her ability to control her emotions around him. Instead, she took a step back and lifted her chin, speaking in her best professional tone. "I'm disappointed we haven't found the killer, that's all."

In the darkness, Wes's headlights caught a couple of sets of shining animal eyes as the SUV bounded along the backroad toward the remote group of cabins in Mammoth Springs. He parked near the door, but left the vehicle running, and allowed relief to fill him.

He hadn't been sure if moving would make a difference when it came to protecting Harlow, but he knew for certain that remaining at the Old Faithful district where she had been attacked was no longer an option. Still, he could feel the danger creeping closer to her, and he might have to move her again and often, or at least until they caught the man after her.

The serial killer.

God, please let us catch this monster.

Remaining in the cab of the SUV, he shifted to Harlow, who appeared less than certain about their new arrangements. She slowly turned to him, her eyes wide at first. Healthy fear was good, he reminded himself, as long as it didn't interfere with her ability to do the job.

"A ranger—Kelly Alexander, if I remember his name correctly—was supposed to meet us here. Obviously he's not here yet." He squeezed the steering wheel. "We'll wait a few minutes."

He let the lights shine on the cabin while all around them the darkness seemed to close in. Through the woods, though, he spotted security lighting and inside lights on in cabins. They weren't completely secluded. Still, in the light of day, moving out here had seemed like a good idea.

"Can I ask why I haven't seen the National Park Service investigative agent involved? Seems like he or she would be all over this investigation."

Her question seemed kind of out of the blue, but maybe not. "Oh, Agent Jeffers is involved, working the case from a different angle. They invited us to take the investigation. The task force was formed, and I was asked to lead." He hadn't meant to share so much, though it was no secret.

"Wes... I hope you don't mind my asking, but honestly, I was surprised to see you here."

"I didn't hear a question in your statement, but you were no more surprised than I was to see you again."

"When we were back at the academy you were...an overachiever, and I mean that in the warmest way."

He chuckled. "Okay, I'll bite. What are you getting at?" But he thought he already knew.

"No...never mind."

What? "Go ahead and ask, Harlow. I mean you've already insulted me, what's one more insult."

She gasped. "I had no intention of insulting you. I just imagined you heading up some big-city field office by now. So that's a compliment, isn't it?"

He smiled. "It is, thank you. I'll answer your unspoken question. I was up for a promotion to SSA—supervisory special agent—in fact, in the Portland office. But my mom had a stroke. An agent retired in the Cheyenne office, and so I took that position instead so I could be close to her."

"Wow. I'm... I'm so sorry to hear about your mother. How is she doing?"

"Much better, thanks."

"You're a good man, Wes."

Her words warmed him to the core, despite her earlier words that he was an overachiever. She'd spoken the truth, but with Mom's stroke, he'd questioned why he worked so hard. "I worked with Dad in his office before going to college. Did you know that?"

"I think you told me, but you never said why you became an FBI agent instead."

He rubbed his jaw—he'd have a beard before this was over at this rate—and stared out at the woods, watching in the mirrors. His father had been a judge before becoming a state representative, and his mother had been a lawyer but retired a decade ago. Dad kept on working, though. "I worked with him on campaigns while getting my degree in political science. He always expected me to follow in his footsteps. But I developed a distaste for politics and resisted his demand that I attend law school. I had no intention of becoming a career politician."

"I understand, but why the FBI?"

He could ask her the same question—and he would at the right time. "My father needed protection. Someone was targeting politicians, and the FBI was involved and saved his life. That was the day I saw clearly what I wanted to do with my life. Make a real difference."

"So you were accepted and went to the academy, where we met."

He nodded, his throat thickening so he was unable to speak. His career had taken off in meteoritic fashion, and he'd liked to believe that his success had everything to do with his work ethic and not his father's political influence. He scraped a hand through his hair. Sure, he was a workaholic and liked to push the envelope, skirt the edges of the rules to get things done.

That was then.

And this was now. He glanced at Harlow, who stared at the cabin ahead—their accommodations for tonight. Was he still skirting the edges of the rules? Was that what he was doing in keeping her with him?

He wasn't sure. But he knew that he'd

been on the cusp of a promotion, and he'd given up the dream of that more prestigious position for family. For love…a decision he'd never imagined he would face.

Life was made up of hard choices. Like now. He needed to get out of this warm cab and leave behind this almost heart-to-heart conversation with beautiful Harlow, because concern for the expected ranger crept into his bones.

"Stay here. I'll check it out first."

"What about the ranger?"

"He'll be here, but I'm not waiting anymore. Stay in the vehicle. Leave it on and the doors locked."

"Look, I know you're in charge here, but I'm a cop, too, so let me do my job. Let me help."

He sighed. She was right. "Then let's do this."

He extracted his gun, as did Harlow, and they both climbed out. Inside the cabin, they cleared the rooms and then moved to clear the outside as well.

Lights flickered along the drive, and Wes waited, ready for anything, as another vehicle pulled forward. He recognized the park ranger's vehicle and let the tension flood out of him, but not completely.

Ranger Kelly Alexander got out and rushed around. "Sorry I'm late."

"I decided not to wait."

Harlow walked around to the back. "I'm letting Nell out for a bit."

Ranger Kelly watched her. "What else can I do to help?"

"You can check in, drive around the area every half hour or so. Will that work?"

The man shrugged. "Normally, no. But under the circumstances—" he leaned closer, and kept his voice low "—with an alleged serial killer out there, it'll be no problem. What about the rest of the task force?"

"Two members are in the hotel at Tower Junction." There hadn't been enough rooms at Mammoth, so they were now spread out. The Old Faithful Lodge had more availability for accommodations, but they couldn't stay there.

The ranger crossed his arms. "I'm working through the night with a couple of others, so we'll keep an eye out."

"I appreciate your help."

Harlow had gotten Nell out and started for the woods, but she hesitated and then directed Nell closer to the cabin.

He held the ranger's gaze. "Good idea to keep her close to the house. I'll go with you."

"That the cadaver dog I've heard about?"

"Yes."

"I'll wait around until you guys get inside. Then I'll check the perimeter."

"I appreciate it." Wes joined Harlow as she let Nell sniff around and take care of her needs.

It felt strange protecting Harlow as if he was on protection duty.

Lord, am I making a mistake?

He led Harlow and Nell into the cabin

and then, with Ranger Kelly's help, moved their duffel bags and laptops inside as well.

Hands on his hips, Kelly glanced around and smiled. "Enjoy your stay, folks."

As if they were just a happy couple on a vacation.

The ranger gave a nod as he shut the door behind him. Wes locked and bolted the door, then made sure all the windows were locked and the blinds shut.

He found Harlow curled up on the small sofa with Nell, sound asleep.

Wes started a fire with the wood stacked next to the mantel. The cabin had two rooms, but he didn't have the heart to wake Harlow up. He settled into a chair, his gun next to him on the side table. This arrangement wasn't any more sustainable than the last place, but tomorrow was a new day.

He could make it through tonight.

The next morning he woke to Harlow coming inside with Nell. He bolted upright, grabbing his gun. "What are you doing?"

"Nell needed to go out."

"We agreed, Harlow. You agreed I would go with you everywhere, if you wanted to stay on the task force."

Her gaze flitted around the cabin then landed on him. He recognized her pure panic. He hadn't thought she would break his one rule so soon.

"Relax. I left the door open, and we were just right there. I could see you, Wes. I just…didn't have the heart to wake you. You must be exhausted. Did you sleep last night?"

He glanced at his watch. "You should have woken me up. Now we're late."

"You canceled the meeting this morning, remember? We're all to check in with you and report separately."

He dragged a hand down his face.

Harlow approached with a half smile. "I know I could use some strong coffee. How about you?"

"Yes." He scratched his itchy jaw. He could use a shower and a shave, too, but he was already starting the day late. "Let's go find some."

Nell was in her crate and Harlow and Wes had gotten in the SUV and buckled when a text came through. He read the text and his heart sank.

"What is it?"

"A park ranger talked to someone who thought they'd seen suspicious activity in the area."

"Suspicious activity?"

"A man with a shovel hiking from the woods. They didn't get a good description of him because they only saw him from the back." He held her gaze. "Time for Nell to go to work again."

Her expression grim, she nodded. "We're ready."

He plugged the coordinates into the GPS for Lone Star Geyser. "It'll take us half an hour at least to get there."

So much for strong coffee and a clear

mind. Protecting Harlow, worrying about her, was taking its toll.

Wes would meet the challenge and win. Failure was not an option. This was not a training exercise at the academy.

Real lives were at stake, and Wes was prepared to stand in the path of a killer to save them.

EIGHT

Wes parked along the forest road near the trail that would take them closer to the Lone Star Geyser. The Firehole River gurgled close by. With the fresh morning air, a cool breeze, and the risen sun...all of it belied the danger lurking.

Harlow and Wes got out and he opened the back of the SUV for Harlow. Nell's big brown eyes stared at her with such intensity, it was as if the K-9 sensed that she was about to make a discovery.

While Harlow wanted to find Cassidy, she didn't want to find her dead. Dread filled her gut as she released Nell from the crate. She curled her fingers into the dog's fur and spoke softly to the beagle, her coworker and...really...her pet. She loved Nell, cared for her whether she did her job or did it well.

Man's best friend.

In this case, woman's best friend. Harlow keenly felt Wes watching her as she rubbed Nell behind the ears, but this time, she didn't attach the leash.

"Time to go to work, Nell." She eyed the dog. "You ready?"

Nell whined eagerly and licked Harlow's face.

"That's what I thought." Harlow spared a glance at Wes and wished she hadn't. Something shiny sparked in his eyes and warmed her insides. "Are you ready? She directed the question to Wes and offered a half grin. "Time to keep up with my dog."

He nodded. "Let's go then."

She assisted Nell down and gave the command for the beagle to search for remains.

The K-9 took off running northwest, and Harlow followed her. Wes kept a few paces behind Harlow. Nell slowed and pressed her nose to the ground, sniffing as she continued moving northwest, then she changed course and moved away from the direction of the Firehole River and toward the geysers to the west.

Wes remained close and seemed as eager as Harlow to see if Nell alerted on anything, but she also felt the protectiveness rolling off him. Such a different experience from when they were so competitive back at the academy, but Harlow found she appreciated the fact that he had her back, and they were working together, even in the middle of what felt like an intolerable situation. Being the focus of a psychopathic killer left her feeling unnerved, but she had to push past that and do her job.

Nell kept moving through the area, past a thicket of trees then nearer to the geothermal pools. She circumvented the pools and headed toward a wooded area near the river again.

The dog raced forward and left them behind. Harlow hadn't grown winded yet and so picked up her pace. She heard Wes running behind her to catch up with her K-9. Heart pounding, she knew deep down that Nell had indeed picked up the scent of death. When she caught up, Nell had stopped and was nosing around pine needles that had clearly been pressed over disturbed ground, then Nell sat.

That was the signal that she'd found human remains.

Harlow crouched. "Good girl." And gave Nell her treat. She leashed her up, then led her a few yards away from the spot. She was so proud of her girl.

Wes got on his cell and called for assistance at the spot where Nell had alerted. Still, though Harlow was glad that Nell had located remains, her heart sank and her gut soured at the thought they might have finally found Cassidy Leidel. No one wanted to find the ranger dead. No one wanted to find her buried.

A half hour later, the rest of the team had gathered with them—the sheriff, park rangers and task force members. Bill and Perry started to work on the area to which Nell had alerted.

Chills crawled over Harlow again as she swept her gaze around to catch Wes watching. Everyone held the same grim look as they each scrutinized the shallow grave being so carefully excavated.

Whose body would they find? At times like these, she thought back to the reason she'd decided to handle a cadaver dog. She'd wanted to bring closure. But the moment a K-9 discovered remains brought with it a kind of torture of its own—any hope that a loved one was still alive faded with the discovery.

At the approach of footsteps, her peripheral vision saw that it was Wes, but she didn't look at him. She'd known it was him, of course. He'd barely left her side since her near abduction. And when he did...he was maybe five yards away.

While law enforcement was here, Harlow wasn't in danger, so she figured he would give them both some space. But now? Wes stood close enough she could smell his woodsy masculine scent. *Oh, please don't stand so close.*

He inhaled long and slow and released the breath.

She finally glanced at him. He appeared to watch the techs gather evidence, working the ground with their tools and bags, but Wes's demeanor told her he was very much aware she studied him. His palm remained near the weapon in the holster at his side, like he thought someone would jump out of the woods at them. He had that air about him, and she expected him to say something, but he remained tense. Maybe he couldn't find his voice.

She got that. She hadn't found hers either.

The two techs stood.

"They found something...*someone*," he said under his breath.

Together, she and Wes headed over to look at the remains...a body.

Finding it took her all the way back to the day when she was twelve. The remains of bones that she'd found. She would never forget that day.

It had impacted her entire life.

Harlow turned her back on the scene before her emotions got the better of her and led Nell away. She refused to let Wes or any of the others witness her complete lack of control. Hadn't that always been her issue? She thought she'd gotten on top of it by now. But something about searching for a serial killer affected her in ways she couldn't imagine.

Wes stepped up next to her.

He remained quiet for a few breaths, then said, "It's Cassidy Leidel."

Oh Lord...why?

They'd wanted to find her, hadn't they? But not like this.

Not like this.

"While they finish up, let's go get that black coffee." Wes urged her toward the trailhead.

"I don't think I can stomach breakfast."

"I didn't say breakfast. But I'm going to need coffee. We'll meet with the team again after this new development." Wes scratched the almost-beard on his jaw. "We're getting close, Harlow, and that's thanks to you and Nell. We couldn't have found her without you. I told you that you're vital to the team and to finding what we can now call a serial killer."

Her throat grew tight with confirmation of the news they had all anticipated.

"According to his MO, he would already have gone to the next park. Why hasn't he moved on?"

"I think we both know why." He squeezed her arm and didn't let go until they were at his SUV.

He opened the back for Nell and they went through their usual routine. When Harlow was done, she lingered on Nell longer than necessary, working up her nerve. Then she turned to look into Wes's handsome face and snagged on his disturbed gray eyes that had turned darker than usual. Intensity poured from them. Finding Cassidy seemed to have changed everything, especially the atmosphere around them.

He stared at her long and hard. The way he took in her face... Her throat closed up. Mouth went dry. Her future was in his hands, and she feared his decision. "You and Nell were the stars today, Harlow. I hope you'll consider staying until we finally catch this guy. We need you."

She'd been sent specifically by Tyson to search for the remains of the missing park ranger. Now that job was done. But she heard what Wes was saying loud and clear—that this man was a serial killer and he had targeted her, and though she would be safer in Denver, he *wasn't* asking her to leave.

He took a step forward. "I know you're capable of protecting yourself, especially now that you're being so vigilant. But with a serial killer after you, I won't let you out of my sight."

"I know. And, yes, I'm staying. I want to catch this guy." The fact that she and Nell had proved themselves and were needed was all she could hope for.

Relief welled up inside, but it was tempered by the fact that she was very much still in danger as long as the killer was out there.

Later that night, Wes was relieved the long day had ended, except it was far from over. He finished clearing the cabin they'd moved into last night at Mammoth Springs, but he wouldn't breathe easier, not really, until the killer was caught. He hadn't been able to get the image of Cassidy's body out of his head—all day.

Harlow was feeding Nell and petting her dog, loving on her. She appeared to draw comfort from Nell, and the beagle from her. He understood that need for comfort, but at the moment he had no one in his life. No friend or even a furry friend that he could hold close.

Harlow had removed her ponytail and her blond hair hung over her face as she knelt near Nell. She finally settled on the floor, putting her back against the sofa and her legs straight out. Her eyes drifted from Nell over to where he stood at the kitchen counter. Such big, beautiful blue eyes.

How did he make sure that no one ever tried to hurt her again? Yes, they needed her in the investigation, but it was within his authority to send her back to Denver. He could bring in another handler, though that would take additional time he didn't want to waste. Harlow was here, and they were getting closer to catching this killer. Was he doing the right thing by keeping her in Yellowstone with him? Was there some dark ulterior motive deep inside that had him keeping her in the region so that he could draw the killer to him? The thought disturbed him. No. That couldn't be it.

Scratching his itchy jaw, he moved over to the table and pulled files out of his briefcase, along with the laptop.

Harlow got to her feet and approached the table. She arched a brow at him. "You're exhausted, Wes. You need to rest."

Fighting a grin—this was not the time to smile—Wes stared at the file he'd dropped on the table. He never could have imagined this moment—staying in a log cabin together so he could protect her. Her telling him to get some rest. She was right but...

"I can't sleep."

"Me neither." She left him there and headed to her room, but returned with her laptop, pulled out a chair and sat.

Wes opened his own laptop.

Harlow rubbed her temples and stared at her screen. "There's so much information running around in my head, I can't think straight."

Wes appreciated her knowledge and skills. She was FBI trained, after all, and an experienced law enforcement office before adding cadaver K-9 handler to her résumé, which only made her that much more important to their investigation.

"I understand. I wish we could take a break to clear our heads, but there's no time."

"He's out there, looking for his next victim." Her voice sounded strained, but he heard something else.

Determination.

He admired that about her, and he felt equally determined, but he still wouldn't voice his thoughts, his fears, about the next intended victim being Harlow. He wouldn't let that happen, which was the real reason he couldn't sleep. He would request additional security tomorrow as well as move to a new location.

But tonight, they would work. "I should tell you..." He tapped his fingers on the table. Why? Why did he need to tell her?

He lifted his gaze to look into her beautiful blue eyes. Before it was too late, he needed to tell her. "When you showed up that first day, I... I was frustrated." He rubbed his forehead. "There wasn't any getting around the fact that we had our issues working together."

She opened her mouth to speak, but he held a hand up.

"Please let me finish. I want to say I should have known that you would be amazing. You quickly proved yourself, but really, you didn't need to. I'm sorry about what happened before..."

She hung her head, that blond hair covering her eyes, then she angled her face so it fell away. Half her cheek hitched in a grin. "Isn't that the past we're supposed to forget?"

"Yeah, that past." He returned her smile. "I guess I was just a young, cocky aspiring agent."

"You had every reason to be. You were the one who was amazing...and still are."

He leaned his head back and looked at the ceiling—the log trusses—then at Harlow.

"I'm not so sure now, after landing in Cheyenne." Should he really be that open? That vulnerable that he would speak his fear about his career...something he hadn't even admitted to himself?

"Don't doubt yourself. I mean...you were on a roll there. Going places. Everyone knew that. And you know what? They still know it, Wes."

She'd been on that same roll back then. Now look at them. She held his gaze, the color in her irises deepened.

And that reminded him of their tumultuous romance. The shared kisses. He hadn't forgotten *that* past. Oh no...he remembered all right. He remembered the softness of her lips, her kisses. And somehow they'd continued with their competitive rivalry. At first, it had been more about fun, but then it had grown serious and gotten out of hand.

He rubbed his eyes. Oh boy. He had better steer the conversation in the right direction—except Harlow spoke first.

"So you're a special agent out of Cheyenne now instead of SSA in Portland because your mother had a stroke. Where do you see yourself in two years or five?"

"You sound surprised that I would refuse a promotion. Why? You don't think I would shirk my family responsibilities, do you?"

"What about your father? Isn't your mother his responsibility?"

"Yes, but he's been traveling, preparing for the upcoming election." He frowned. "And I'm traveling too. But I plan to resolve this case quickly before someone else is hurt."

She slid her hand across the table, hesitated and then pressed it over his. "We'll find him, Wes, don't worry."

She held his gaze captive, and Wes was powerless to pull his hand free. All the what-ifs of their relationship from the past collided in his head.

"I sometimes wonder what would have happened if things had been different eight years ago." A blush rose in her cheeks and she slipped her hand back to her laptop.

Had she been reading his mind?

They both knew they simply couldn't revisit the past—the bad that had happened—for obvious reasons.

And the good that had happened. Again, for obvious reasons. He couldn't go through the pain and agony of a broken heart a second time, and that's exactly what would happen because he already knew he was no good at relationships.

Time to redirect the conversation. Again. "When Nell found the remains...it affected all of us, sure, but you got quiet. I'm curious—was your reaction somehow different than other remains you and Nell have found?"

He didn't know how or why, but he sensed that it was. And maybe he just knew Harlow too well.

Even after all this time.

NINE

How did the guy know? Had she done such a poor job of hiding her reaction? Wes apparently knew her moods too well and could read her expressions, her emotions. Not good. And their late-night conversation was getting far too personal for their own good. Or, at least, her own good. But she'd wanted to understand about why Wes had taken a different course in his career path. And now...now he wanted to know what was behind her reaction to finding those remains. Finding human remains was what she and Nell did. That was their job, and Cassidy's remains certainly weren't the first she'd ever found or seen, or else she wouldn't even be here on this investigation.

"I...yes. Finding Cassidy hit me harder than usual."

He angled his head, compassion and curiosity in his gaze. "Why do you think that is?"

How did she explain?

She wouldn't tell him all the reasons why, because she hadn't quite figured those out yet. Some of it had to do with the fact that she was much more involved with this investigation, even going with Wes to question Harrison and Barnes. "Honestly, in general, it hits me hard every time."

"But you already admitted this time was different."

She pursed her lips and stared at the laptop screen. She hadn't booted up the computer yet and pressed the power button to do so. "I'm not sure why. It could be that I'm closer to this investigation than I have been in others."

He nodded. "That's fair. But I've been wondering something else since you got here."

"Oh yeah? What's that?" Tensing, she pressed her finger into the biometrics button and her desktop appeared. What could he possibly want to know now?

"I told you how I landed in Cheyenne," he said. "How about you share how you ended up going from the FBI academy to cadaver K-9 handler for the RMKU."

How much should she tell him? "Well, as you might have guessed, our battle of wills in front of our academy classmates left me embarrassed. Though, indirectly, that started me looking at other options when I had been singularly focused on working for the FBI."

Regret tugged the corners of his mouth down. Did he blame himself? This conversation was becoming uncomfortable, and she feared that the hurt and anger might ignite again. She couldn't let the past ruin their newfound working relationship.

He started to speak, and she suspected another apology was forming on his lips.

Clearly, he'd handled that argument much differently.

"No need to apologize. What happened sent me in a different direction, that's all. And it was the right direction. I love what I do, Wes. I wouldn't have it any other way. But I won't go as far as to thank you and our argument for that." A small laugh escaped.

"Okay, so you went another direction. And?"

"What more is there to tell?" Okay, well, a lot more. "I ended up working for the Santa Fe PD, which makes sense since I'm from Santa Fe. You know how it is—doors open and you walk through them. I got into K-9 work then moved to the RMKU when invited."

"Right. That all makes sense. But why cadaver, specifically?"

So he was going to dig deep. She sent him a wry grin. He knew her well enough to know there was much more to the story. "That's personal."

She risked a glance at Wes and saw the hurt. And it pinged through her heart. "I... I'm sorry I said that."

"No, it's okay. I didn't mean to pry. It's none of my business."

But she'd just given herself away and admitted that her reasons went far deeper than what she'd revealed. They'd been working together so well, despite what had happened before—the argument and the breakup. By the ache in her heart, Harlow had to admit she wanted Wes to know the deeper truth. With the admission she realized, too, that their relationship before had only been budding, but had remained superficial. They hadn't gone deeper then. Oddly, now working together in a time crunch and pressure cooker situation, they were learning more about each other than they had at the academy. She wished she knew what it all meant.

Despite his claim that he didn't mean to pry, he studied her as if waiting on her answer.

"I *want* you to understand." She wasn't able to look into his gray eyes for long and instead chose to watch Nell sleeping soundly on the floor as she told the story. "It's kind of strange I never told you this before."

He pushed his laptop aside and leaned forward on the table, clasping his hands.

Okay, he was all-in, and she wasn't sure this was worth his time, but...

"When I was twelve, we bought an old house in order to renovate it. At that age, the only thing I could really do well was swing a sledgehammer into the Sheet-rock, so that was my job." She might have laughed at her comment, but morbid images accosted her and she squeezed her eyes shut.

"It's all right, Harlow, you don't have to tell me if it's too hard." The tenderness in his voice went straight to her heart and chiseled some of the protective wall away. And, oddly, she wanted him to break it down. If anyone was going to do it, she wanted that person to be Wes.

"I want to tell you." She'd planned to tell him before. "Just...give me the time to process through it as I talk."

He said nothing more, but by now his imagination might be going in all sorts of directions about what she might say next.

"I found...a skeleton...in the walls." She glanced at him. Concern and again...tenderness...hooked her. She couldn't look away. "Imagine a kid finding a skeleton in the walls."

He reached over and took her hand in his, reassuring her. She could tell he wanted to say something, but he pursed his lips. He would let her finish without interrupting.

"I remember staring at the bones of a small child. The horror of it nearly choking me. I wanted to scream but I couldn't. I remember my dad shaking me, pulling me away from the wall and against his chest. Then I screamed. I don't know when I stopped screaming."

"I'm so sorry," he said.

"Oh, it was bad. I had to sleep in the bedroom with my parents for weeks. Saw a therapist. You mentioned earlier that handling a cadaver dog is not for the weak... I feel like I've earned the right to be here, if that makes sense."

He squeezed her hand. "What happened next?"

"Oh...right." She slipped her hand from his and pulled her hair into a ponytail. A nervous habit—and telling this story definitely made her nervous. "I was a kid, you know? Kids need to know that monsters aren't real. That skeletons aren't going to pop out of the closet or walls. So it took some time for me to get over it. A few years later, I learned that the bones belonged to the owners' daughter from three decades before. It wasn't until after they had moved out of the house that their young daughter had gone missing, and they never found her. The exact reasons for her death and being in the walls isn't known, but murder by a neighbor is suspected. The neighbor was the reason they had moved to begin with. He had become fixated on their daughter. Looks like he took her, and then after he killed her, he simply hid her body in the walls of the empty house. All involved parties are dead."

"That's quite a story, Harlow. You've been through a lot."

"You wanted to know why cadaver dogs. Well, seeing the skeleton in the wall traumatized me. And then later, when we learned about the girl in the walls, it really stuck with me. That family missing their daughter and never knowing what had happened to her. That was something I couldn't get over. So I wanted to bring closure somehow. Bringing closure to others helped *me* to process through what I found."

"And you got your degree in psychology, then joined the FBI."

She nodded. "At first I thought about becoming a therapist, but then I decided I'd prefer to be part of the investigation process. So, yeah, the FBI. Then the PD... And then, when the opportunity to be a K-9 handler—a cadaver dog handler—opened up... I knew that was the right place for me, and I could bring closure to families, after all."

As if sensing Harlow was talking about her, Nell crept over and nuzzled her leg. Harlow ran her fingers through Nell's fur and around her ears. "Working with Nell gives me a great sense of satisfaction. Though it can bring pain, it also brings resolution."

She once again looked at Wes and caught the admiration in his eyes.

"And as painful as the news is, at least now we know where Cassidy is."

Tap, tap, tap.

The sound came from the window. Heart

hammering, Harlow stiffened. "What's that?"

Wes grabbed his gun from the table, his expression focused and determined. He handed off his cell. "Call Ranger Kelly and get him out here."

Harlow brandished her gun as well. "What are you going to do? What's the plan?"

"I'm going to check the perimeter. You stay here, quiet and hidden." He eyed the gun in her hand and leveled his gaze on her. "And shoot to kill."

God, please let it not come to that.

Wes calmed his heart and steadied his breathing. He was an experienced agent and though Harlow was an experienced police officer, his commitment to protect her ramped up all the fear. Adrenaline surged and took over so he could act quickly and think clearly.

Holding his gun at the ready, Wes turned off the inside lights but left the security lights on outside, then he stood back to the wall near the window and slowly peered out, searching for the source of the tapping.

"What do you think made that sound?" Harlow whispered the question from across the room.

"I wish I could say that it was simply a branch hitting the glass. There's a good breeze out there and I see branches moving. But no trees are close enough to hit the window or the roof."

"Are you sure?"

"Not completely." But the tapping had sounded...intentional. He ignored the dread growing in his gut. "I'm not going to check the perimeter until Kelly gets here. Someone could want to draw me out to get to you."

"Then let them come," she whispered. "I have a gun and I know how to use it."

"Of that, I have no doubt." She was trained FBI and a police officer, after all.

"Then let's do it. Wes, this could be our

chance to get this guy. If he's out there, let him in. Between the two of us, we can take him down."

Had she so quickly forgotten the close call from before? Granted, she hadn't been expecting to be abducted and now she was ready and waiting, but he wouldn't take the risk.

Fortunately, headlights shone between the trees as a vehicle approached the cabin. "Help is on the way, so we don't need to wait."

"Already?"

"Kelly said he would make sure someone was close by in case we needed help, considering the dire circumstances."

"You mean circumstances surrounding a serial killer on the loose."

"Exactly. Yes, you've got skills, Harlow, but considering the threat to you, I need you to get behind the kitchen counter. I'm going to open the door. When I close it, lock it behind me, then get back into a secure position."

She said nothing and Wes took her silence as agreement. He carefully opened the door just as the truck lights were cut, but he could see a ranger stepping from his vehicle, his weapon out and at the ready, his posture menacing. Another set of headlights appeared and tires crunched along the drive. The additional vehicle parked next to the first ranger's truck. Another two rangers hopped out.

Kelly approached Wes. "Someone tapped on the window? He's here then?"

"He could be. Or he could have fled already. But I need a perimeter check. I'll take one of you with me for that. The other two can stay here and guard Harlow." *With your life, please.*

Kelly gestured to the female ranger. "This is Ranger Gayle Johnson and Ranger Toby Cooper."

The woman stepped forward and Wes led her to the cabin and opened the door. "Harlow, Gayle is coming inside to wait with you and protect you."

Harlow emerged from the darkness with a slight frown. Maybe she didn't like the protective arrangement, or they seemed like overkill. He appreciated how seriously Kelly was taking the situation. The ranger understood that the faster they could shut down a killer in the national park, the better for them all.

"I'm Harlow. Nice to meet you. Sorry to drag you out—"

Wes shut the door on their conversation. Toby braced his gun and stood next to the door. Wes nodded at Kelly, who would go with him to check the perimeter and clear a wide swath around the cabin.

Holding his weapon in a low ready position, shining his flashlight, Wes crept around the cabin then moved to the woods. Kelly mimicked his movements a few yards away.

"What was that?" Kelly whispered. "I heard something."

They stood motionless. Waited and listened.

Wes heard something all right. Behind them. He whirled to stare at the cabin.

Gunfire erupted from inside. Heart pounding, Wes raced back to the cabin, Kelly on his heels.

A figured sprinted out of the cabin into the woods on the opposite side. Kelly gave chase and Wes started to follow but... Harlow. The cabin door remained flung open. Morbid images flashed through his brain.

Gayle stumbled out of the cabin, holding her head and her gun. "I called 9-1-1. Toby's hurt. I got a shot off, but the attacker escaped."

Wes pushed passed Gayle.

Harlow knelt on the floor next to Toby, pressing her hand against his shoulder. She looked up at him, a mix of fear and determination. "I'm okay. But help me save him."

Wes rushed to her side to help her. Kelly was out there alone, chasing a madman, but at least the ranger wasn't the intended target, like Harlow. "What happened?"

He glanced between her and the door when Kelly returned and joined them, along with Gayle and a medical kit. Park rangers were first responders, trained as EMTs because the nature of their jobs took them into remote locations. Kelly flipped on the lights and Harlow and Wes moved aside. Gayle dropped next to Toby and started addressing his wound.

"You're going to live. We got this," she said to the man.

"What happened?" Wes asked again.

"He… He came through the window."

Wes glanced over and just now noticed it was broken, as if he'd simply dived right through it.

"Gayle and I both had guns," Harlow told him, "but it was dark. Toby rushed inside and got stabbed. The guy tried to take me, but Gayle got off a shot, and he took off."

"Do you think he was hit?"

"I don't know, but likely."

"And then I lost him in the woods,"

Kelly growled. "We can get people out in the woods to search for him tonight."

Wes looked at the ranger. "It's too dangerous. He's a killer. We know he's out there, but he'll have blended in with other campers by now." He hated that he bit out the words. But Kelly had to know Wes was frustrated at the situation. Not with the rangers but that, despite there were four of them here tonight, a killer had once again almost gotten his hands on Harlow, and the killer was ramping up his efforts. "I appreciate your assistance and how quickly you showed up."

His expression grim, Kelly said, "I'll assist Gayle getting Toby into the truck—and she probably needs to get checked out, too—but we need to transport him, as soon as we get him stable, to meet the helicopter. Then I'll come back and help you guard the cabin for the rest of the night in case he comes back."

After everything that had just happened, that was asking far too much. "That won't be necessary. We're moving." Besides, this was a crime scene now. Somehow the killer had followed them again. But then, once he had his target, it probably wasn't that hard to follow them. He'd only needed to pay attention to the agents and task force and the ranger activity. This guy knew his way around parks.

Wes grumbled under his breath as he watched Harlow wash her hands of the ranger's blood, then move to the sofa and grab Nell into her arms, pressing her face into the dog's fur.

God, how do I protect her and find a killer?

TEN

Nell nudged Harlow awake with her wet nose.

"Go away. Let me sleep."

Harlow rolled over and Nell whined. Early morning light streamed through a crack in the blinds, practically screaming at her to get up when she wanted nothing more than to sleep. But she also wanted to act like a professional and knew she shouldn't sleep in even though they'd had to move last night.

Ugh. She hadn't gotten to bed until after three.

She'd wanted to be on this task force, but she couldn't wait until the nightmare was over. Her cell buzzed and she lifted it to look at a text. She cracked one eye open and tried to read the message, but her vision was blurry.

From Wes? Why hadn't he just knocked on the door? Oh. Maybe he had and that's why Nell was trying to wake her too.

I'm sorry to wake you but we have new developments.

Shame flooded her. He was up already, and things were happening without her. And worse, he'd had to wake her up.

Harlow rolled out of bed and quickly dressed, wishing she could take a long shower to wash away the grime. Opening the door, she stumbled out of the bedroom toward the kitchen and the fresh pot of coffee, the aroma drawing her in a beeline. She didn't acknowledge Wes or even look at him but was well aware that he watched her from the table where he sat, laptop open.

Please don't speak to me.

She might growl at him.

She poured a cup, sipped on it and stared out the kitchen window at the beautiful view. They'd moved to new accommodations near Tower Junction in the middle of the night, the move facilitated by the rangers. While she appreciated their help, if the killer wanted to follow them, it would have been easy. There was no getting around this issue. No real safe house in Yellowstone. They just needed to catch the killer. *God...please...*

Wes approached from behind. She rubbed her eyes and weaved her hands through hair that she'd forgotten to brush before turning to face him. Harlow hated the fact that she probably looked horrid, especially looking up into Wes's face—how did the man appear so put together, so bright-eyed and so handsome at this hour after the night they'd had? Still, he had a few more lines around his eyes she hadn't noticed before, and he had neglected shaving. Again.

What would it feel like to kiss him and

feel his rough face? Heat flooded her cheeks and she turned away, hoping he hadn't witnessed that. But he seemed to catch every one of her emotions and moods. Every nuance. And if that was true, then what must he think of her?

Nell whined at the door. Oh right. Her dog needed out. Harlow was grateful for the distraction.

"I'll take care of Nell," Wes said. "You finish your coffee and get ready. It's going to be a long day."

That went without saying. "Deal. But what's the new development?"

"A woman's missing."

Harlow needed more coffee. "Blond hair?"

He nodded, adding, "Blue eyes."

"Where?"

His jaw worked. Why couldn't she stop looking at it, admiring the sharpness, the angles, the strength?

"Mammoth."

Gasping, Harlow dropped the mug and it

shattered, the remaining hot coffee spreading across the floor. "Wes… I'm sorry."

Heart pounding, Harlow glanced up at him and held his gaze. "Mammoth? As in Mammoth Hot Springs? We were…we were just there."

What does it mean? She grasped at the answers racing through her mind, not wanting to grab a hold of any of the possibilities.

"He came after you last night, Harlow. But he…" Wes pursed his lips, pain in his eyes. "He couldn't have you so…" He was unable to finish.

She didn't need him to finish. She knew what he was going to say. Neither of them could voice the words. Covering her mouth, she held back the sobs. The ridiculous, wholly unprofessional sobs. And just like that, Wes scooped her up into his arms, holding her against his chest like she weighed nothing at all, startling her.

"What? What are you doing?" She wasn't so fragile she would break over the news. Or was she? Maybe he saw that about her and she refused to admit it.

His jaw was much too close as he looked down into her eyes, his gray gaze turning to steel. "I didn't want you to cut your feet. We don't need any distractions."

Distractions could lead to mistakes. People could die. But despite their best efforts, people were still dying. As for distractions, Wes was definitely distracting her.

She was barefooted and shards of the coffee mug had scattered across the floor. He could have carried her out of the kitchen and put her down, but instead he held her longer than necessary, and Harlow didn't mind. She didn't mind at all. Caught up in his nearness, the ropy sinews of his muscles, his broad shoulders and hard chest, Harlow couldn't breathe. She slowly pulled her gaze from his lips and back up to his eyes, which had turned from steel to emotion-filled pools.

Her heart pounded. *What am I going to do?*

Nell barked.

Wes carried her over to the table and away from the kitchen, then released her.

"Let me get shoes on and I'll clean up my mess." She headed for her room.

"You get ready for the day. I'll clean it up after I walk Nell. I'm not taking her beyond the door. We need to stay alert."

And wary.

At the bedroom door, she paused. "Wes, what's her name?"

"Janine Norris. A geology student." He leashed Nell.

Brandishing his gun, he disappeared through the door.

Harlow's heart was heavy with thoughts of the missing woman. Better than thoughts of the attraction surging through her when Wes had whisked her out of the kitchen and held her close for a few seconds longer than necessary. She needed to forget that feeling of being held by him, protected from the small danger in the kitchen, but nonetheless protected.

And cherished.

In his arms, looking in his eyes, she felt like he cherished her. She had no business thinking of him in such terms, and even if she did have business thinking of him like…well…like they were a thing again, which they weren't, another woman had gone missing. Guilt suffused her that she was so easily distracted by Wes when women were disappearing and dying.

Lord, please help us stop this killer!

And please…let Janine still be alive.

Harlow had to continue hoping, just like she had with Cassidy, though Cassidy had been murdered, after all. Tears welled as she grabbed a quick shower—not the long one she wanted—and changed into clean clothes. She brushed out her wet hair and secured it in a ponytail. Pulling the door closed behind her, she stepped into the main cabin and Nell rushed up to her. Wes was pulling a bag from the garbage, presumably holding the broken pieces of the mug.

"You're done already?" She hadn't taken that long to get dressed.

"All done."

"Good. I'm going to grab another cup of coffee and I promise not to drop it. Then we can get to work. What do you need me to do?"

Wes set the sack on the floor and moved to gather up the materials spread out on the table. "We'll grab breakfast and head to the facilities—the Canyon Lodge and Cabins—where we'll meet with those on the task force who can make it. Everyone else can video chat."

He snatched up his cell when it buzzed and answered the call. Harlow watched his expression remain serious. "Text me the location. Thanks for letting me know." He ended the call.

The lines in his face relaxed.

Interesting. "What's happened?"

"Good news. Janine escaped."

She sucked in a quick breath. "What? That's great news, and seriously amazing that she got away. But how?"

"We're heading over to question her now. We'll grab breakfast to go and eat on the way. Get Nell loaded up."

Shock rolled through her though the news was good. It was still hard to believe. Harlow nodded, elated that Janine had survived. "Maybe she can tell us what we need to know so we can finally identify this jerk."

And boy would she like to get her hands on him, but she buried those thoughts. Vengeance didn't belong to her.

"Let's hope so." He dipped his chin, held her gaze. "This could be the break we need."

God, please let it be so.

Hope fueled the bounce in her steps. They were getting closer to catching the killer. She could feel it in her bones.

After locking up the cabin, Harlow secured Nell in the back of the SUV. Wes assisted her, never leaving her side, his demeanor always tense and protective so he never let down his guard. He was especially intense when they were surrounded by woods, like now.

A shiver raced over her back.

Was the killer watching her from those woods?

Tension corded his muscles, tightened his neck as he steered them down the two-lane curvy road through mountains of Yellowstone National Park and toward the designated meeting place. Harlow was texting on her cell and he was glad she was distracted so he could mentally process what had happened—all of it.

Things were picking up pace now and he didn't like that the increased criminal activity of a serial killer had everything to do with Harlow, or at least it seemed that way to Wes.

Last night, a man had tried to abduct Harlow at the cabin—with FBI and three rangers there to protect her. They'd assumed it was the killer, and Wes would go with that. The killer had wanted to get to Harlow enough to try it with two rangers guarding her.

He already knew the man was a psychopath, but his desperation told him just how dangerous this guy was, and that he was willing to go to crazy lengths to get what he wanted.

He'd been unsuccessful at getting his hands on Harlow. So…what? He takes another woman in her place?

Was the killer taunting them? Taunting Harlow? Trying to terrify her? Well, she held it together and put on a strong, determined front, but he suspected she was terrified.

Because deep inside, Wes was terrified. He couldn't let that get the best of him or reveal it to those he led, or the killer would win. But he couldn't deny that the threat on Harlow's life had increased exponentially. He felt like this guy was breathing down both their necks.

Had Janine really escaped or had the killer let her go? He wouldn't know the answer to that until they were able to question the woman who was in protective custody—until this was over. No one knew if the killer would make more attempts on Janine, like he had on Harlow. Wes reasoned the guy had come after Harlow multiple times because he didn't like that she had thwarted his plans, and he wouldn't give up. He could come after Janine again as well. But, clearly, he was losing his ability to abduct women, or at least to keep them until he could kill them.

On the one hand, that was good. He was making mistakes and would soon be caught. On the other hand, he could change his MO and instead of abducting women, he could kill them on the spot.

The thought soured in his gut.

Lord, help us stop him!

Janine had been transported to a lodge on the lake at the south end of Yellowstone and the drive would take them more than an hour. Harlow continued to stare out the passenger window at the spectacular view, rubbing her arms now and then, as if chilled. But Wes knew her reaction had nothing to do with the colder weather that had moved in with a storm front.

"We're going to get him, Harlow." If only he sounded more convincing.

She shifted from the view of the forest, steam rising off geyser basins, to look at him. "Do you truly believe that?"

Her question surprised him. Before he answered, he measured his words. Did he believe it? Harlow would want the truth from him and, at the moment, he wasn't sure what he believed.

Except this one thing. "We have to have faith, Harlow. We have to believe we're going to get him, and we can't let any doubt creep into that belief. I've seen how determined you can be, so let's do this together. Stay determined and finish this."

Once and for all.

Together. They made a good team.

He tossed her a momentary glance to catch the raw relief in her eyes as she gave a slow nod. Then she turned to face forward, and her eyes widened.

"Watch out!"

He slammed on the brakes as a herd of buffalo streamed onto the road. "Well, that's just great."

She chuckled.

"I don't think this is funny."

"Well, I do, and it's far better to laugh at the situation than cry." She grinned.

He couldn't help but return the grin; admittedly, they needed levity in this morbid investigation. "Is that your mantra?"

"I say it all the time."

"Do you find yourself in a lot of situations in which you could cry?" Oh, now he wished he hadn't said those words. She'd cried quite a bit during this investigation.

"Yes. A person has to have a sense of

humor or they'll go crazy. And, come on, you know we need that now so we can survive this, and yes, stay determined and believe we'll get him."

He stared at the buffalo, willing them to keep crossing and get on with it. "I know you're right."

"I've been thinking."

His turn to chuckle. "I'm not sure—"

"Don't even say it."

"Say what?"

"That my thinking wasn't a good idea." Amusement danced in her tone.

"You know I'm only teasing." Because, really, she was as sharp as ever. "So let's hear it."

"We talked about the psychology of serial killers before, briefly. You gave me a crash course."

"I wouldn't call it that."

"We already know that Martin Barnes and Harrison Cahn have many of the characteristics in common with serial killers."

"Right. Cahn spent his childhood going from one foster home to another."

"Plenty of people have those characteristics who aren't killers, of course. They're just struggling. Those are the kinds of people that Cassidy was helping in her old job and even, apparently, on the side because she was a good person."

Wes heard the pain in Harlow's tone. The emptiness. "You're a good person too, Harlow."

Why had he said that out loud?

"Thanks. Um…"

"You were making a point with this when I interrupted." She was getting under his skin. Correction—she was already under his skin. Again.

"The other day, during some downtime, I made a few calls. That text I took a few minutes ago? Well, I heard back from a lead I followed."

The buffalo had started moving from the road and Wes shifted into gear and slowly drove forward, glad they were traveling again, but he was more interested in what she'd learned. "I'm listening."

"Barnes was put on a seventy-two-hour psychiatric hold a couple of years ago," Harlow said.

"Really." Why hadn't they already learned about this? But Harlow was on the task force, too, and they had all been assigned with looking for all leads. "Good work, Harlow."

"In the psych report, he tried to commit suicide. Was still upset an entire year after his fiancée, Cara something, left him. The details are being emailed to me. Sorry, I can't recall her name at the moment."

Interesting.

"Do we have any additional information on his fiancée?"

"Since my main purpose here is to work with Nell, I thought I would bring this new information to your attention. I can try to contact Cara and talk to her. I would have brought this up earlier, but it just came through."

"Find out if she has blond hair and blue eyes. I'd like to know if she's still living as well."

"That would tell us something, wouldn't it?"

"It would be circumstantial—as in not enough evidence to convict him—but yes, it would tell us something. We'd know more about what had set him off if he's our killer."

Finally he turned down a road that would take them to the lodge where Janine was staying—at least long enough for him to question her. He'd been told she would be leaving Yellowstone altogether after their interview.

He escorted Harlow and Nell into the lodge. The inside had the predictable stuffed wildlife on the walls and the smoky smell of a large fireplace. He led Harlow down a long corridor to a door where two county deputies—not law enforcement rangers—stood guard. Wes suspected that was because the sheriff's department would be the ones to escort Janine from the park to a safe location. Wes flashed his credentials and entered the room to see the woman whom the serial killer had abducted.

Seeing her—the same blond hair and bright blue eyes as Harlow—nearly knocked the breath from him.

ELEVEN

Harlow stepped into the spacious rustic suite behind Wes, and at the sight of Janine Norris, who sat at the dining table, her throat constricted. Janine wrapped her hands around a large steaming mug. Determination surged in the woman's red eyes, then her gaze locked onto Harlow. Slid down to Nell, who never failed to draw attention, especially in her K-9 uniform, though Harlow wondered if the sight of a police dog would be upsetting to Janine, given the circumstance.

Still, Harlow released her empathetic beagle, who really doubled as a therapy dog. Nell ambled over to Janine in that friendly dog way of hers, though her tail didn't wag. She seemed to understand this meeting wasn't one of joy.

The hint of a smile spread across Janine's features as she slid her chair out and reached to pet Nell. "Well, hello there."

Heart flooding Harlow with compassion, she joined Janine at the table. She briefly glanced at Wes—after all, she didn't want to interfere with his interview technique. He gestured with a nod that she should continue.

"What's her name?" Janine asked.

"This is Nell." Harlow didn't elaborate on Nell's special skills as a cadaver dog, which would definitely change Janine's relaxed expression. "And I'm Harlow."

While Harlow focused on Janine and Nell's response to her, she remained aware of Wes's actions. He'd moved to the counter where two other law enforcement officers stood, one of them was a sheriff she hadn't met before, and he offered Wes a cup of coffee and gestured at a display of pastries. Wes declined the coffee, his gaze flicking to her.

For a few minutes, Janine ran her hand along Nell's fur.

That's right, Nell. Help Janine to relax. Yep. Therapy dog.

If they ever retired from police work, she might end up being a therapist after all.

Harlow returned her focus to Nell and Janine. Her beagle appeared to enjoy being the center of attention, and also giving comfort, which was an important skill in Harlow's book. Janine twisted in her seat and gripped the mug again, signaling she was finished petting Nell. The beagle moved a few paces to lay down by Harlow's feet.

Jeanine stared into her mug. "I know you're here to ask questions. Thank you for giving me a few minutes to get my emotions in check. I'm glad you didn't need to use her—I mean she's a search-and-rescue dog. Or a tracker."

Fortunately, Wes chose that moment to

approach them, and Harlow didn't correct Janine's assumption.

Wes sat next to Harlow, in the seat across from Janine. "Thank you for agreeing to speak to us. I'm Special Agent Wes Grey."

"Sheriff said you're heading up a task force to catch this guy." Janine lifted her eyes to study Wes.

"Yes."

Emotion—Anger? Frustration?—flitted across her features. Harlow got the sense the woman worked hard to hold back an outburst.

"Since you escaped him, we're hoping you can give us details that will help us prevent him going after someone else."

Janine vigorously shook her head and stared into her mug again—a focal point to help her rein her thoughts. "I didn't see him, I'm sorry."

Disappointment shot through Harlow, and she noticed Wes's shoulders drop slightly. Janine hadn't given them the answer they'd hoped for.

God...please...we need something. Please let her remember something that can help.

"No need to apologize." Wes's tone was gentle and caring. "Please, take your time and tell us what happened."

Wes flicked his eyes to the sheriff then back to Janine. She'd already told him the story and would now have to relive it as she shared the sordid tale with Wes.

The woman nodded and lifted her chin, as if gathering her courage.

"It was early morning. Twilight really. Dawn hadn't broken when I was on the top terrace and taking notes. I usually hike up all those steps to enjoy all of the springs, but I decided to park at the top instead this time. I love the quiet of morning before the tourists get out. My only warning was a disturbance of a flock of birds. I thought—" a tear leaked out the corner of one eye "—I... I thought it was just elk or some other animal that disturbed the birds."

"So you weren't worried or scared?"

"Not at all."

"What happened next?" Wes asked.

"I heard something, but before I could turn, someone grabbed me from behind, covering my eyes with a cloth." Janine shuddered and struggled to continue.

Chilling memories of being accosted from behind—each time—flooded Harlow. The second attempt to abduct her, someone had tried to put something over her head. The third time—in the cabin—she hadn't seen him then either. The lights were out... Grunts and groans as the ranger fought with someone... She couldn't see to shoot... Before she knew it, the man had run away... She could relate to Janine's frustration—why couldn't they catch this guy?

Because if they didn't get him soon, more women would suffer or die, and this guy had showed that he was targeting Harlow. How long would *she* survive?

"Then what happened?" Wes urged Janine to continue.

Janine released the mug she'd gripped so tightly and stared at her shaking hands.

"He tied my hands. I couldn't see, of course, but it felt like he used a leather strap."

Creepy.

Harlow remembered the shoelace found at the disturbed ground the day she and Nell arrived. "What about a shoelace?"

"No. Wait…maybe. I don't know."

A shoelace from a hiking boot maybe. Boot prints had been found outside Cassidy Leidel's window.

"Could it have been a bandanna over your eyes?"

Harlow felt Wes's eyes on her, but she didn't look at him, fearing she might see disapproval. This was his interview, after all.

"I'm not sure. Sorry."

"I think we're getting ahead of ourselves." Wes shifted forward.

Harlow couldn't ignore him and looked his way as she sat back in her chair.

"Can you tell us how you got free?" he asked.

Eyes welling with unshed tears, Janine sniffed and nodded. "He got a call, and that distracted him. He hadn't tied my ankles yet, if that's even what he intended. But he released me to answer the phone. I fell to my side and played dead. I mean, he's a dangerous predator, and that's what we often have to do in those cases, right? I was able to rub my head against the ground to remove the cloth and then see where I was going. He had his back to me, so I scrambled around my car then took off into the woods, not all those steps. I thought I could hide in the tree line, so I just kept running until I made my way down to the edge of town where someone untied my hands and got me to safety. We called for help."

Sobs finally escaped, mixing with laughter and a smile. "I can't believe I survived. I'm just…so grateful. Thank You, God."

"Yes, thank You, Lord." The sheriff spoke from behind. Looking at the grim set of his jaw, Harlow got the sense that he was feeling antagonistic toward their efforts to catch this man. Janine had survived due to no help from them.

"Can you tell us anything else?" Harlow asked.

She wiped at her eyes, took in a few shuddering breaths then nodded. "When I ran away from him and my vehicle, I spotted something shiny, something flashing, on the roof of my car—like the sun had caught it just right."

"What do you think it was?" Wes asked.

"I...a knife. Yes...that's what it was. A knife." Janine paled with the words.

The day before she was killed, Cassidy Leidel had taken an oversize knife away from Harrison Cahn. But like Wes said, that was only circumstantial, considering how many Yellowstone campers kept knives of all sizes. It meant nothing, really.

"Janine, you've been very cooperative, and we thank you for your time. Please contact me if you remember anything else, no matter how small." Wes slid his card across the table.

Janine stared at the card. "I will."

"Know that we might contact you again if we have more questions."

Once they'd said their goodbyes to the sheriff, and Janine petted Nell one more time, Wes and Harlow exited the room. He headed down the hallway. Harlow and Nell could barely keep pace with him.

"Wes, hold up."

He paused and turned to wait for her to catch up. His gray eyes had turned darker than she'd ever seen.

Chills raced over her.

"Two women have escaped him now," he said.

She heard what he hadn't said.

The killer is angry, and more determined than ever.

Wes tried to push down the rising fear that the killer's frustration with not getting his hands on Harlow seemed to lead to increased attempts on his part. Harlow was in danger, but other women were in increased danger as well, as if the threat hadn't already been serious.

Disappointment that Janine hadn't seen her abductor lodged in his gut and pulled him down like a weighty anchor of defeat. She'd been able to escape and run for help, and he didn't blame her for not waiting around to see who this guy was. But it rankled none the less.

He led Harlow out of yet another lodge and slowed his pace so she and Nell could match his stride as they made their way to his parked SUV. He hadn't meant to come off so gruff, and he hoped that she understood where he was coming from.

She hadn't said anything; keeping quiet, allowing him to work through his frustration.

Once Nell had been secured and he and Harlow were back in the SUV, he started the engine, turned up the heat to take the chill out of the gray day that reflected his mood. No. His mood was much darker than gray.

"We should talk about this," Harlow said.

Talk about what? His mood? How disturbed he was? Or her personal fear? "To which 'this' do you refer?"

"The big white elephant in the cab of this truck."

There could be several of those elephants, so he wouldn't go first. "I'll let you talk about it."

"Okay. Well, it seems obvious that the killer is escalating his abductions. I'm concerned he could change his tactics too."

"It seems he's changed already by choosing to stay in the park after Cassidy and not moving on. In a way, that gives us the advantage, so we don't have to wonder which park he's going to move to. I agree, things are escalating."

And I'm terrified for you.

Wes shifted in his seat. He didn't trust himself to drive at this moment. In the past, during their academy days, Harlow had been the one to struggle to control her emotions. Now Wes found himself working overtime to keep the emotions—the fear and panic—out of the way so he could focus and make good decisions. The outcome of this case would of course affect his promotion opportunities in the future, but that was the least of his concerns.

Lives were at stake.

He shut his eyes and rubbed his temples, showing his anxiety a little too much. Harlow needed to believe in him, especially after his "have faith" speech. He was letting himself down, too, not just her.

"Say something, Wes. I can tell how much this upsets you. I'm upset too. I mean I'm relieved that Janine escaped, but that maniac could be out there right now trying to abduct someone else because Janine escaped. Because I escaped. Shouldn't the authorities clear the park? Close it?"

"Yes. There's a strong possibility that

will happen." Wes would confirm with his superior that was their next move and then work with the National Park Service to close Yellowstone. But it wouldn't be fast enough, considering the killer was no doubt prowling for his next victim, and more than determined to succeed this time, after his failures.

"But if they do," she said, "he'll only move on to the next park, which isn't good. But at least we've done all we could to save lives."

Had they done all they could? *Is there something I'm missing, Lord?* "Until that happens, it appears he'll stay in this area and try again."

"Agreed. And that's exactly why I'm going to let him target me again."

Wes struggled to comprehend her words. They slammed into him. "What? You mean bait him? Are you out of your mind?"

"Excuse me?"

Furious, he gripped the steering wheel

though he wasn't driving anywhere, for which he was glad. "I don't think my choice of words is too strong here. That's an emphatic *no* to your suggestion. Baiting him is absolutely out of the question."

"I wondered how long it would take for us to finally disagree. This is just like old times."

Had she really just said that? A hundred retorts crossed his mind but Wes bit them back. "Look…emotions are running high. You and I aren't the same people we were at the academy. We were young and inexperienced. If anything, our disagreement now is the complete opposite of what it might have been then. I was the one to push the edge of the envelope, and you were the one to follow the rules. Don't change on me now, Harlow. I need you to be who you've always been—a fantastic investigator and a stickler for following the rules."

"How am I breaking rules? My suggestion doesn't push the edge."

He didn't trust his next words and, unable to respond, simply shook his head, incredulous. Ready to end this discussion, because there was no discussion as far as he was concerned, he started the engine, shifted the SUV into gear and backed out of the parking lot in time to spot the arrival of a National Park Service investigator and another local deputy. Coming to move Janine to a secure location until this was over, likely.

"Where are we going now?"

"Back to our accommodations. I'm calling a meeting of the task force this evening." His palms slicked against the wheel. Wes had never been an agent to grow nervous about his investigations, but the sweat beading at his temples belied his confidence in the outcome.

Harlow pressed her hand against his biceps, sending a supercharged current up his arm and to his heart. He fought not to respond or shift away. He had to maintain his composure.

"You're doing great, Wes. You're the one to lead this task force. We're going to get this guy. I have a feeling about that. But you know that the closer we get to nailing him, the danger and tensions increase, and it's to be expected."

She dropped her hand, and he instantly felt the disconnection. Wes had the strongest urge to stop on the side of the road and pull her into his arms. He'd tried to ignore the feelings that he obviously still harbored for her—after all, this wasn't the time or place, nor was it professional—but the fact that she was at increased danger seemed to wipe away all his filters.

He flipped on the radio that played a local country station, because he needed the distraction. The silence between them filled with anything besides his tumultuous thoughts. By the time they arrived at the lodge, he'd cleared his mind and calmed his heart.

He helped Harlow get Nell out and stayed with her as she took the dog for a walk in the designated area. He didn't like that dusk was setting in.

She tilted her head and her blue eyes shimmered with an emotion that took his breath away. Trust. She trusted him. That made sense—he was the lead agent on this task force, but he knew that trust went much deeper. Because—he swallowed— yeah, the trust had mingled with longing.

He would love to turn the other way right now and not look at her graceful movements, her shiny, wavy hair. Her delicate but strong hands as she tenderly cared for her dog.

K-9 cadaver beagle.

He reminded himself that Harlow was a tough police officer and worked well in the RMK9 Unit. He shouldn't be thinking about her in any other terms. Then again, that knowledge only increased his admiration for her.

She smiled up at him as she closed the distance, leading Nell toward him, though he had only been a few yards away. Not too far at all. But she drew even closer than necessary, studied him, then frowned. "It's been a long few days, Wes, and you got no sleep last night. In fact, when was the last time you got a good night's sleep? Getting some rest will help us think clearly."

What did she see when she looked at him? He had to appear haggard, a look that probably didn't instill confidence. "I don't have time to rest. Not yet. I have to get ready for the meeting—" he glanced at his watch "—in half an hour."

Concern for him poured from her eyes as she nodded but then suddenly seemed to realize she was standing too close. She abruptly stepped back. Her heel caught on a branch, and he grabbed her to prevent her from falling and then steadied her. The simple act seemed to glue his hands to her, so he couldn't let go.

"Harlow... I..." *I want to kiss you.*

She tipped her chin up, bringing her mouth closer, as if in answer to his silent plea.

Wes gently brushed his lips against hers,

and the sweetness that was Harlow swept through him, settling in his heart.

I shouldn't do this.

He didn't want to hurt her again. Hurt either of them. What was it about this woman?

God, why did You bring her into my life again?

Just when he thought to bring her closer, pull her against him and kiss her thoroughly, Nell barked.

The sound jarred him, and Harlow stepped back, clearly as startled as he was. Wes grabbed his gun and they both glanced around.

"Do you think he's here?"

A ranger hiking through the woods gave a pseudo salute when he spotted them. Nell barked at him again then whined.

Harlow picked her up. "I think we need to go in and get ready for your meeting."

She was right. He wanted to apologize for his actions, but maybe they both needed time to think about them. He wouldn't be guilty of regretting his words this time.

He walked next to her in silence back to the lodge and prayed the killer hadn't quickly located her again. They'd gone the extra mile to be careful. But he couldn't seem to put to rest her earlier words. They clung to him, feeding the growing dread.

I'm going to let him target me.

TWELVE

After the task force meeting, Harlow was finally alone and in her room. She needed to sleep, but that seemed impossible. The meeting had felt like it lasted forever as they went over the same information repeatedly, everyone hoping to see something they'd hadn't seen before and somehow missed. Harlow had remained attuned to every single word as she'd fought the memories—still fresh—of Wes's kiss.

Or had that been *her* kiss? Completely aware of what was happening between them, she'd lifted her face and asked for it, hadn't she? *Idiot!*

But they'd both been more than willing participants in what never should have happened.

She plopped down on the bed and stared at the log ceiling. Wes was on his cell. She could hear the rumbling timbre of his voice. But at the same time guarding her. Protecting her.

And what else? Something else was going on between them besides work and protection.

Even as she agonized over her proximity to her love interest from the past, she thought about the kiss. Closing her eyes, she relived that amazing moment. The feel of his hands as he kept her from stumbling, and then he didn't let go. Oh, she hadn't wanted him to let go. She'd longed to be wrapped in his arms and, as if answering her heart's desires because Wes had shown himself great at reading her mind, he'd pulled her closer and kissed her—tenderly, but in that one kiss she sensed all the longing, all the deep emotion, he still held for her. And she held for him. She didn't think any of it had dissipated over the years and, if anything, she felt more for him now. She knew him deeper. Had worked with him well.

What they had now…in just a few days… was more than they'd experienced back then over weeks.

Years ago, a lifetime ago, it seemed, they'd had a romantic relationship and shared a lot of kisses. But tonight's kiss was different. Very different. Was it that she just couldn't accurately remember those kisses from long ago? Or was something different with him now? Or her? The both of them? And that made more sense if that was the case, but she didn't think this emotionally deep kiss had anything to do with the changes in them as people.

This one gentle kiss—though the tension had been held in check on both sides, she was sure—held promise. Tenderness and emotion had touched her heart. That must be it. He'd found a way past the barriers she'd erected, some of those barriers due to her past with him.

Deep regret gripped her. All her thoughts and wishes were a waste of time. It could never work between them. They'd started this way, after all, when they'd met at the academy. She'd been instantly drawn to his charisma and that feral look in his eyes. Those intense gray eyes had pulled her in right from the start. Theirs had been a whirlwind romance until the academy training intensified and their fierce competitive natures had turned them into rivals. What was to stop that from happening again? Their competitive natures setting them at odds against one another? That had almost happened tonight—she wanted to work this investigation a certain way and had offered a suggestion, and he had refused. She'd seen the proverbial writing on the wall. Eventually, they would be at each other's throats.

It can never work.

Harlow closed her eyes again.

Remember that. Do not let him get under your skin.

She needed a plan. An escape from having to work so closely with him. This investigation should end soon. Then would she still be working with the RMK9 Unit? She could use a good distraction and glanced at her watch. Good. Not too late to call Tyson. Talking to him about the very real possibility that the RMKU contract with the FBI could be up in November sobered her mind and heart. She didn't feel like they'd been given a long enough chance to prove they were needed.

She pressed the contact listing and Tyson answered on the second ring.

"Hey, Harlow. I'm glad you checked in." But he didn't *sound* glad to hear from her. Something was bothering him. "I was just thinking about calling you."

She pressed her hand against her midsection as concern rippled through her. "Oh? Have you got news for me?"

"I'm afraid so," he said. "Though I really can't say what it means."

What a way to tease her, not to mention his tone scared her. "Can you please just tell me?"

"Right. You're right. I don't like having to say it, but I've received an official warning. SAC Michael Bridges arranged a formal meeting in a few weeks."

Tyson might lead the RMKU but he reported to Bridges since they were under contract with the FBI. There had been too many incidents plaguing the RMKU over the past several months, and Tyson's leadership had been called into a question.

But a warning? What did that mean exactly? She was afraid to ask, but she could assume the worst. "I... I don't know what to say." *I'm devastated?* "I've learned so much from you." This wasn't all about her. "And I know you've invested your heart into the RMKU. Do you really think he's going to end the contract? You've done phenomenal work, managing our team.

How could the FBI not want us involved?"
Okay. Now she should just stop talking.

Her anger flared at the FBI.

Wes. He was FBI. Good. She could be angry at him, though the decisions made regarding the RMKU had nothing to do with him.

Tyson blew out a long breath, clearly as distraught as she felt. "I appreciate your vote of confidence, Harlow. Let's not jump to conclusions yet. This isn't over. Still, I felt I should share with you what's happening. I could be reading too much into this formal meeting."

You mean warning.

"Maybe Michael hadn't intended it to sound like a warning, and I shouldn't have conveyed it that way to you."

"I understand. You're good to us, Tyson, and wanted to give me a heads-up so I wouldn't be blindsided."

"You got it. Now, I have news for you on the missing baby case."

Harlow sat up and swung her legs over

the edge of her bed, listening intently. His tone had shifted to something more positive, holding hope. "Oh good. What's happened?"

"If you recall, Kate Montgomery, the woman found unconscious outside her burning car near the empty car seat and baby blanket, is still in the rehab center."

"Right. How's she doing?"

"The good news is that she's getting some memories back."

"Wow. That's great news. Has she remembered anything that will help?" Harlow stood and paced the small space.

"I know why this case means so much to you, beyond the fact it's regarding a missing baby, of course."

"Thanks. I appreciate that." In her interview, she'd shared with Tyson the reasons behind her working with Nell and the need for closure. The bones of a child she'd found in the wall. This missing baby affected her more deeply than others, and that was saying a lot.

"She remembered the last time she'd seen Nikki Baker."

Okay.

"And, Harlow, the next piece of information is also part of the reason I was about to contact you. You beat me to it."

Her? Why would Kate's case have anything to do with her? "I'm listening."

"Kate can't remember details of why the baby, Chloe Baker, had been in her car. But she does recall that the last time she saw her friend, Chloe's mother, Nikki Baker was a blonde."

"I mean…yeah, we knew she'd been wearing a wig but…" A heavy gasp escaped. *No!* Dread settled in her gut. She eased back onto the bed that creaked and wished the small space had a chair too.

"We didn't initially associate her disguise with the case you're working now, and it just hit me there could be a connection, so I wanted to keep you informed."

"I'll inform Wes right away."

"Thank you," Tyson said. "Everything

we learn, no matter how small, can help us. We all have our smaller investigations, but they can be tied together in the bigger picture of criminal activity."

"Agreed. Anything else you can tell me?"

"The police told Kate that Nikki was wearing a wig when she was found dead in her car in that ditch, but again, Kate doesn't remember why her friend needed a disguise."

"This just gets better and better."

"Indeed," Tyson conceded. "Unfortunately, we don't think we'll find the missing baby—until Kate gets her full memory back."

And the news cut Harlow to the core. She prayed that a cadaver dog wasn't needed to find Chloe. "Poor Kate, she must be so worried."

"As we all are."

Harlow released a heavy sigh.

"Let's hear about your progress on the serial killer case."

She shared the details up to today when they'd met with Janine Norris. "We all feel that we're getting close. Nell found Cassidy Leidel's body, and Wes feels like we're close to finding the killer, thanks to Nell."

At the words, chills crawled over her arms and she rubbed them.

"Harlow...you need to be careful. Very careful." She heard the fear in his words, and what he didn't add.

He's come after you three times now.

She ended the call, guilt pinging through her heart. She hadn't told Tyson everything. Nothing at all about the working relationship with Wes...or the more personal side. Of course, she wouldn't tell him that.

The cabin where they stayed remained eerily quiet, and Wes would normally be grateful for the peace and quiet, except every creak of the logs and every scratch of a tree limb against the window had him on edge.

God, please let this be over soon.

He'd been up all night. Pacing. Watching. Guarding. Listening. And this setup with Harlow was killing him. Literally eating him up inside. He was exhausted, for one thing.

But he had to hold himself together just a little longer and he knew that he could do it. He'd done it before on many occasions. They were going to get this guy. He could feel it in his bones. Though walking around exhausted wasn't helping anyone. Not him. Not the task force. And certainly not Harlow.

The thing was, he was all about protecting her while they simultaneously hunted this guy. But he also needed to protect her from someone else.

Himself.

Why. Did. I. Kiss. Her?

What kind of leader kissed someone on his team?

Okay, well, maybe one that had a deeply personal past with said team member. Still, was he so pathetic and weak, he couldn't have kept his distance from Harlow for just a little longer? Though he berated himself, memory of her in his arms broke through and washed away his recriminations.

He paced again. Glanced out the windows at the darkness surrounding them. Protecting her and working with her under these circumstances was pure agony. His mind was scrambled in a way it should never be as a professional, especially in the middle of an investigation involving a serial killer. He scraped both hands across his face and through his hair.

What should he do now? What was the right thing? How was it he had no idea?

At least he'd talked to Tyson earlier, and they'd discussed the abduction attempts, and the fact that her gun had been taken. Wes had reassured Tyson that she was under Wes's protection, and that he also had full faith in her abilities, but so far things had not gone as planned. Wes had hoped the call to Tyson would ease his own mind, but he remained unsettled.

He quietly eased onto the sofa. He had to get sleep. That was it—he was just too exhausted to think clearly, especially when it came to Harlow. Wes set his watch alarm for three hours, then closed his eyes, his gun within easy reach. Unfortunately, her words from earlier grated against his thoughts, causing his neck and shoulders to remain tight.

I'm going to let him target me.

Was he wrong to stop her? She was strong and capable, and maybe, at the end of the day, that was the only way to catch the killer. After all, the maniac wanted Harlow. Instead of giving the killer a reason to go after another unsuspecting victim, instead of sleepless nights and constant pacing, looking over their shoulders, maybe Wes should let Harlow do her job as a police officer and stop trying to be overprotective.

That was hurting their investigation.

He feared, too, that she might find a way to bait the killer on her own, and though foolish, if that happened, it would be on Wes. He couldn't let that happen. It would be better to support her decision, observe and provide backup, than to risk her trying to go it alone. Though he didn't truly believe Harlow would be that foolish, he couldn't risk that she might.

Peace finally settled over him.

For the first time in hours—days, even—he felt like they had a solid plan. He'd refused to consider the obvious. Tomorrow he'd inform the team and they would make plans to lure the serial killer into their trap. Wes wanted to share his decision with Harlow first, of course, and see the reaction in her eyes, but it was best they both got some rest.

Tomorrow would be a new day and they would stop this killer once and for all.

Wes started when his watch went off. He could have slept longer and had forgotten he'd set it. But he'd get up and make coffee.

Communicate to the team that they needed
to talk at eight this morning. Since it was
six thirty, he had some time to gather his
thoughts to present the plan. He'd talk this
over with Tyson too, to get his input. But
first, coffee. He made it strong and black,
just the way she liked it.

What was he doing playing house?

They weren't married. Not even a couple. But the thought of making her coffee—in their own home, them together,
flooded his soul.

He poured a cup and then tapped lightly
on her door. "Harlow, you awake yet?"

Nell whined and barked.

He smiled. "Sounds like Nell's ready for
you to be, if you're not. I can take her out."

Today was the day they were going to
get the killer. He felt it to his bones. "Harlow, you decent? I made you coffee. I'll set
the cup on the table and open the door so
Nell can come out."

Nell's leash was on her crate in the middle of the room. They didn't bring the

crate in every time, but Nell often chose to sleep in it, and Harlow was good to her dog. Still, Nell had stayed with Harlow in her room last night.

After setting the mug on the table, he cracked open the unlocked door and Nell rushed out, barking. He crouched to love on the dog like he'd seen Harlow do so many times. Crazy images of a white picket fence, a home, a dog and cat, and Harlow...the thought took his breath away. What was he doing? He stifled the anger, the grumble that rose in his chest. He wouldn't be angry at himself for wanting a life. But now wasn't the time.

"Come on, girl. Let's get you leashed up."

He'd just finished with the leash when the door behind him creaked.

A sleepy-headed woman peered out. "What are you doing?"

She rubbed her eyes, her blond hair askew. Adorable. In a weird way, this reminded him of Christmas morning. She dropped her hands and yawned. Blue eyes took him in and seemed to finally register he was taking Nell out.

He smiled and stood. "What does it look like I'm doing?" Maybe that question was too much this early and before coffee.

Starting with his feet, her eyes looked him over until they finally landed on his face, his eyes.

"You look...different." She took a step toward him. "What's going on? Did we... did we get him?"

She sagged as if reading his expression.

"Not yet. But soon." She'd read far too much in his expression and mood. He'd allowed his feelings to surface when he should have tucked them away. Hidden them deep.

"I didn't mean to change your mood," she said. "I kind of liked that look on your face. So, really, something's different. What is it?"

Nell whined and paced next to him.

"Why don't you get ready for the day while I take Nell out? Then we'll talk."

This was getting to be a habit with them—him taking Nell out in the morning.

He gestured toward the table. "Uh, I got your coffee."

Another habit...and he would love it to last forever.

Outside the door near the cabin, he held his gun and remained wary while he allowed Nell to sniff around the small area.

What am I doing? He had no business thinking about a more personal relationship with Harlow, especially not now, and probably not ever. In the meantime, he had to focus on a delicate and dangerous operation that would put Harlow at risk and at the same time save her from future attacks. Save her and others.

They were going to get this guy today, whatever it took. He kept that mantra going in his head while he ignored the dread curdling in his gut.

THIRTEEN

Though Harlow finished dressing and secured her hair in a ponytail, she felt groggy and out of it, and couldn't seem to shake the exhaustion. And she wanted to be completely awake for what came next. More importantly, she was more than eager to see what was up with Wes. She smiled to herself as she listened to him talking to Nell in the main room.

He was jabbering on with Harlow's dog like they were best friends. Maybe his actions weren't so unusual, but it felt… well, sweet. She must be reading it all wrong. Her wishful, wrongful thinking. She hoped the kiss wouldn't change things between them and alter the way she perceived every look and every word coming from him. But how could it not change everything?

She needed to go out and tell him she was ready, but he was still talking to Nell, and she loved listening to the soft timbre of his voice. The sound of it, and the fact he was talking to Nell, warmed her heart. Okay, time to go. She rushed out of the room.

He stood then whirled around. Opened his mouth as if to speak. But his jaw kind of hung open for a moment before she finally said, "Looks like you got some rest last night."

"I don't feel like I did, but thanks."

Honestly, she could tell he hadn't, but that didn't surprise her. Still, something in his demeanor was different. She hadn't imagined it earlier nor could she put her finger on it. She'd already downed the first cup of coffee so she scooped her mug from the table and poured another. "Okay, what's going on?"

"Can we talk?"

She leaned against the counter. "I thought that's what we were doing."

He jammed his hands in his pockets and blew out a slow, even breath. This must be big news.

"I'm waiting."

"I'm considering what you said yesterday."

"Which thing?" Her pulsed jumped.

"The thing about using you as bait."

She nearly dropped her mug. Glancing at the floor, relief rolled out of her. She didn't need another one of those incidents. "I... I don't know what to say. What changed your mind?"

Was she just seeing things or did it appear a thousand reasons flashed in his eyes in one moment?

"You were right. We've been chasing this guy for days, only to come in after someone is abducted. We need to turn the tables to have the advantage." His eyes turned dark. "But... I need you to promise me you'll follow my *every* instruction."

Harlow was still trying to comprehend that he wanted to use her idea, but couldn't find the words before he spoke again.

"Do I have your word? No breaking the rules we outline for this."

She nodded. "Yes. All right. If I recall, you're more likely to break the rules."

"I've changed."

I can see that.

"And we're talking about lives here. *Your* life," he added.

"I promise I'll follow our carefully laid-out plan. I guess we'd better get started on this plan." Not in a million years would she have thought he would agree after his harsh reaction to her suggestion yesterday.

"I've already come up with a plan, and I've recruited law enforcement rangers, deputies and a couple of ex-military local police officers. You'll be safe, or I would never risk it."

Wow. Okay. "I think if I'm going to be the bait, I should have some input."

"By all means, I welcome your input."

He stepped back, giving her the space she needed to breathe, then moved to the table. "Come on over and see for yourself."

He opened up his black leather portfolio and revealed drawings. After glancing at his watch, he said, "We're meeting with the task force in two hours."

"How are we going to make this work. I mean really? If I'm alone, he'll know something's up. And if there's too much law enforcement around, that won't work either. We could be making a big mistake. What if he isn't going to target me again, after he failed for the third time and then with Janine."

"We're not giving up on all our tactics, Harlow. The NPS has set up roadblocks to all exits and entries to the park. Only tourists are getting out...at least, the usual way."

"Right, because he could hike out of here."

"The net is closing in on him. And in the meantime, though I hate to think of it, I don't think he can resist trying to get you one more time. And we're going to give him the chance to try but not succeed. We're going to get him."

Harlow listened intently and pushed down the rising bile, her earlier bravado slipping away.

"Hey… Hey… Look at me." He lifted her chin. "Okay, we're not doing this. I can see by the look on your face that you don't want to—"

"Yes, I'm doing it. There's nothing for me to worry about with the measures you've taken. With ample backup watching to protect me. I presume they'll be disguised as park employees, maintenance men, and anything but law officers. Except you…what and where will you be?"

"I'll be with you, like always. I'll wander away when I get a phone call. But Nell will remain at your side." He stepped closer again. "Harlow, I'll be watching you every moment."

She stared up into his face, his eyes conveying an intensity she'd never seen before, and that rushed through her and took her breath away. "Thank you…thank you for believing in me."

He nodded, admiration and respect in his eyes, but then concern filled them. "If at any moment you decide you want out of this plan, just say the word."

She nodded and swallowed the lump in her throat. "Let's go catch a killer."

The sooner they caught the serial killer, the sooner Wes and Harlow could go their separate ways. He searched her eyes and suspected those were her thoughts too. Then again, he didn't have to suspect those were her thoughts—he knew they were, to his very core. She was taking the higher road this time and succeeding, much better than he was, at maintaining control.

He'd lost all of it and must rein in his growing feelings for her and bring his soaring pulse down.

In his heart, he knew her true feelings

were just the opposite, in that she didn't really want to go away from him. He was a magnet for her, just as she was for him. What was it about her? Oh, he shouldn't go there, because he would make a very convincing list. And she was right—at the end of this long dark tunnel of tumultuous emotions—they were no good for each other. He couldn't afford the hurt and pain, nor would he want to hurt her.

Again.

His cell buzzed and he released a heavy sigh, grateful for the distraction. Stepping away from his teammate, he inwardly berated himself for his foolishness and read the text. Time to focus on the task.

"The sheriff, deputies, local officers and rangers—everyone is ready and will meet up with us at the main lodge at Grant Village to go over the plan."

Her eyes turned incredulous. "Grant Village? That's where we met with Janine."

"Exactly. They're maintaining that she is still there, and then you will be there, so our killer should be close. How can he resist?"

"Wait… Janine isn't still there, is she?"

"No. But they have created a ruse to make it look like she is."

"So I'm not the only bait?"

"You'll be out in the open and draw him in."

"I thought the plan was already in motion."

"On paper and via text and email. But you and I both know that we need to run through everything in person. We'll drive up to the lodge."

"And you're not worried that he'll run when he sees all the law enforcement there?"

He leveled his gaze on her. "He came after you in Mammoth, which has a large contingent of National Park employees, including rangers and law enforcement. And I think… I think he's getting desperate." Fear pinged through his chest. "And that's why we need to be thorough, and you need to be at your best."

"I'll get Nell."

On the drive down, Wes wished he could have arranged to meet everyone at a different location, but that would have taken too long since a contingency was already in place, preparing for undercover work to catch this guy. Finally, they made it to Grant Village and Wes stopped in front of the lodge where they'd met Janine.

In the lodge conference room, the sheriff, his deputies and two rangers met with Wes and Harlow and went over the plan to bait the serial killer. Wes had also run the plan by his superior, catching him early this morning. His SAC wasn't a fan of these kinds of tactics. However, in this case, he approved because they needed to take advantage of the fact the killer had remained in this park and wanted to get his hands on Harlow. If Harlow had been a civilian, they wouldn't be using her to draw the killer in. Wes's FBI counterpart,

Ricky Shore, was already working under-cover and hiking his way in from another angle to get in position.

Wes glanced out the window across the lake, willing the killer to come closer so they could capture him. If only the plan didn't involve Harlow. At the end of the conference table, Harlow looked down and appeared to be petting Nell. Wes studied her profile.

Lord, am I doing the right thing? Please protect Harlow and help us catch this guy.

"Agent Grey?"

Wes suddenly realized the sheriff was talking to him, and he'd probably been caught staring at Harlow. But the man had to realize that Wes was measuring his decision to go forward. He stood, as if to dismiss the group. "I'm ready. Let's do this."

"Okay," the sheriff said, "we'll be in position within the hour."

This was happening, and fast.

Harlow stood and drew everyone's attention, lifting her chin in a show of determination. "Look, I want to catch this guy as much as the rest of you, but what if he doesn't show up?"

"Oh, he will." The sheriff's confidence seemed to be contagious as everyone shook their heads and agreed.

"How can you be so certain?" Harlow asked.

Frankly, Wes wondered the same.

The sheriff glanced to Wes. "I'll defer to the task force leader."

Great. "We'll stick with the plan. If he doesn't show up today, we'll regroup and try again tomorrow. In the meantime, we continue to use all our resources to find him and stop him We're coming after him from all angles—" Wes pinned each person in the room with his gaze "—is that understood?"

"Understood," the group said in unison.

Two hours later, Wes walked with Harlow along the boardwalk closest to the trees near the West Thumb Geyser Basin, which was the closest hydrothermal feature. He fought to harness his fears and focus on being the FBI agent, the guy he'd been the day he got here.

Not the guy he'd become after teaming up with Harlow. Sure, they made a great team while at the same time fighting their feelings for each other. Not a good scenario.

But they would finish this today.

Near the hot spring, vapor steaming off the pool, Harlow paused. "Isn't that deep blue and the bright orange just beautiful? Who would have thought the colors would be so brilliant? I just..." She glanced up at him, the blues in her eyes equally as brilliant as the pool. "I had no idea."

And I had no idea how much you affected me before...until now.

But it was too late. She'd drawn the line and he wouldn't cross it.

She cleared her throat. "Sorry. The beauty of this place kind of took me away."

"Now isn't the time. You can be in awe

of God's creation later, after we get him."
He offered the smallest of smiles.

"Right. Maybe."

"Are you ready to do this?"

She nodded. Fear flashed momentarily in her gaze, then she jutted her chin out. "Go. Take your call and move away. I'll walk off to the edge of those woods there."

"Ricky can see us, and two rangers are in place in the woods too." Wes glanced around and spotted a park employee picking up trash near the geyser basin.

Everyone was in place. But the risky part? Harlow had to be alone to draw their killer out.

She was wearing a vest. They all were, including Nell. "Don't take your hand off your gun. Be aware of every moment. Every movement. Everything around you."

"I know what I'm doing."

"I didn't mean to imply otherwise." Wes lifted his cell and started talking as if answering a call. They'd picked a place where their cells worked, at least. He turned his back to her briefly and wandered a short distance. A safe distance. He could get to her. Law enforcement was planted in the woods already and had been in place an hour ago in case the killer approached through the woods.

No one would take down a random stranger walking in the woods—he had to be caught in the act of abducting her. They didn't want him to escape on technicalities. Nor did they want to snag the wrong person while the real killer got away, because he was onto their strategy.

Harlow meandered away from him, Nell by her side.

This scheme seemed like their most expedient and best option for catching the killer.

What seemed like hours later, Wes had tired of the stink of sulfur, and a chill was creeping into his bones. He suspected the same for everyone else.

One of their team spoke into his earpiece. "Dusk is going to hit us soon and he hasn't showed up. Are we ready to shut it down?

"Give it a few more minutes. I'll let you know."

Disappointment lodged in his gut. The killer had an uncanny ability to find Harlow, and they'd worked hard to lose him—as far as she was concerned. Had they succeeded this time? Making their efforts to draw him in a complete failure? Was he out there, even now, approaching another unsuspecting woman in a region of the park that hadn't yet been closed off?

FOURTEEN

Harlow could hear the frustration in Wes's voice over her earpiece. Looked like their plan was going to be a big fail, but she also knew how determined she and Wes were—the whole team, in fact—to keep trying. The killer had come at Harlow several times already, so instead of accepting that their plan was a complete fail, she shouldn't let her guard down and instead remain aware of her surroundings at all times.

Sitting next to her feet, Nell whined.

"I know you're tired and thirsty, girl." Harlow sat on a bench near the hydrothermal site. "I'm tired too."

They'd been out there so long it might be too obvious she was being used as bait.

Come on, where are you? What are you waiting for? Come and get me!

Frustration boiled through her veins. She'd been out here two hours already. She and Wes tried to act like their activity was part of a normal investigation, and had focused on the last place they'd been with Janine. So, really, their activity should appear normal to anyone looking on. It was no different than what they'd done in the Old Faithful district where he'd tried to snag her. She'd almost been abducted there *and* in Mammoth... The West Thumb Geyser Basin was probably even easier for him to sneak through the woods—they were much thicker here, especially around the lake area.

Please, Lord, don't let this be wasted time. Let us catch this guy and keep him from killing anyone else.

The rangers had closed off the region to tourists, so it was only her and Wes, and a few other "fake" park employees.

The goose bumps rose again and the hair

on the back of her neck bristled. Was it her imagination? Or was someone watching? She rose from the bench and subtly pressed her palm against her weapon beneath her hoodie, then softly whistled a song they'd agreed could be heard over the earpiece. It was the signal to let the undercover officers, agents and rangers know that something was up. In this case, she sensed someone was watching, and she didn't think it was her overactive imagination.

"Stay vigilant, Harlow." Though barely above a whisper, Wes's tone was stern. "We've got your back."

Wes was twenty yards off and lifted his cell to his ear as he moved away from her...exposing her—the prey—even more, so the predator would be tempted to take her. And this time, with undercover law enforcement waiting for him, this guy wouldn't get away with abducting her and would fail like he had on other attempts. But his effort and subsequent failure would land him in handcuffs and then prison for a long time.

Half an hour later, nothing had happened and Harlow felt foolish.

I know he was out there.

"Let's call it a day." Wes's voice came over the earpiece again. "We'll try again tomorrow."

Relief whooshed through her. She didn't want to continue this plan into the night. The idea to use herself for bait had seemed like a good one, and the best way to get the killer, but as dusk set in and brought a chill in the air, Harlow was ready to be done. Her bones were cold, and she wasn't sure she would ever warm up.

"Come on, girl."

A ranger and deputy, both disguised as park employees, joined Wes on the other side of the steaming pool. So who had her back on this side of the pool? That chill raced over her again, and this time the fur on the back of Nell's neck rose. The beagle barked and strained at her leash, trying to lead Harlow over to the woods.

Harlow resisted Nell's efforts and redirected her. "No, we're not going that way."

Except her cadaver dog was acting as if she had caught the scent of human remains. Why suddenly after sitting here for hours?

"What's going on?" Wes asked. She glanced at him, still across the pool with the other two, but they appeared to be heading her way.

"Nell caught a scent."

"Do not follow her," he commanded. "I repeat, do not pursue. We're coming to you. Keep walking to us."

"Agreed."

Going into the woods alone would be foolish, so she'd wait for the others and then they could all let Nell lead them. Nell had never acted this way. Had someone been killed today? And the body dumped there for them to find? Unease coiled in her stomach.

Or was their killer—someone with the scent of human remains on his body—approaching, and Nell had caught the scent of death on him?

"It's okay, girl." Though it wasn't okay. Not at all.

Harlow tugged on the leash and started toward Wes on the boardwalk. She saw his mouth move as he shouted into the earpiece at the same moment Nell's bark grew louder.

Then suddenly stopped.

She looked down and spotted a red dart sticking out of Nell's hip.

Panic engulfed her. With a shift in the boardwalk, and the sound of pounding feet at her back, realization dawned and she thought to whirl around—but not before strong arms gripped her from behind. She immediately began evasive moves, tried to headbutt the guy, but he shifted out of the path, was faster, and thrust a knife against her rib cage. "Don't fight or I'll shred your insides right now in front of your friends. Hand over the gun."

Another jab of the knife convinced her. She thought he'd broken through her skin since fire radiated through her in the exact spot the vest didn't protect.

Harlow did as he asked, feeling more than the pain of the knife.

"What did you do to my dog? Did you kill her?" Grief and anger coursed through her, and she wanted to fight him, to get the advantage. But she had no doubt that he would kill her on the spot—the team had already discussed that he would shift his MO and start killing rather than abducting. Did Harlow really want to give him a reason to kill her?

"I don't kill dogs. She'll be okay."

And what about me? But fear had choked her ability to speak, or even to think.

In the dim light of the night sky, she saw Wes and the others racing toward her. She willed them to run faster. Their plan had fallen apart...or was there still a chance he could be caught? Was someone closing in behind them, even now?

All these thoughts raced through her mind as he hauled her into the darkening woods, the knife pricking her. He quickly secured her hands and ankles, yanked off her earpiece and mic, then placed a bag over her head.

His grip, his form, was strong as he dragged her, practically carrying her at the waist as he ran through the woods.

Harlow found her voice again. "Why are you doing this?"

It was the only question she could get out; the only words. Her throat grew tight with fear. But she was better than this. If he wasn't captured by the others in the woods, then she would need to fight her way out of this. Their plan never should have gone this far. Had he already taken out some of the backup rangers hiding in the woods?

Lord, help me.

He laughed. "As if you don't know. You're just like Cara."

Cara. She knew that name.

The stress of the moment seemed to block all her memories. She squeezed her eyes shut—though she was blindfolded already. Where had she heard the name?

Cara...

That's it! The psych report on Martin Barnes. Cara was his former fiancée.

The day they'd questioned him, his hand had shook as he'd drunk from the hydro flask. His *right* hand. She'd hit her first would-be abductor with the lug wrench, connecting with his right arm. That had been Barnes!

Where were Wes and the others? Why hadn't they caught up yet? Finally, the man dumped her on the ground and she wasn't able to stop her fall. Her head hit rough gravel. A road?

He tightened the plastic ties. "Move, and I shoot you with your own gun." She recognized his voice now that she thought about it. Definitely Martin Barnes.

But why had they stopped? Was he going to shoot and kill Wes and the others? Hold her hostage? Then she heard a vehicle door squeak, like it was old and rusty and might fall off. He lifted her as though she were a bag of confetti and weighed nothing at all. She couldn't fight this guy physically, and he held all the weapons, including her gun on loan.

God, please let someone be on the way to take him down, even if I die today...let my death be the last by his hand.

Though, really, she didn't want to become another of his victims.

But she was pretty sure her backup wouldn't have intentionally allowed Barnes to get her this far. She struggled to press down the rising fear in her chest.

I might actually die tonight.

Heart pounding, Wes raced through the woods. Gun in his right hand, he gripped the leash with his free hand as he allowed Nell to lead and guide him through the woods, trusting the K-9 to find her master. The dart had only briefly immobilized her because Wes had pulled it out. He was relieved that she was up and running again so quickly. And maybe he shouldn't be using her now, but he had to find Harlow, and Nell seemed intent on that as well. Though she wasn't a search-and-rescue dog, he trusted she would find her beloved master. He'd seen Harlow release Nell to work without the leash, but he feared he would lose the dog in the woods, or the killer might dart her again or kill her this time.

So he tried to keep up.

"Come on, girl. Find Harlow."

How had this happened? How could this plan have unraveled so completely that now Harlow's life was in danger?

"Spread out! Find her. He couldn't have gone far with her!" he shouted, though everyone still had their earpieces and mics.

He and all those who'd come out of the woods—on his calling the operation off—had left Harlow unprotected. Inwardly, he skewered himself and berated them for their poor handling. It all fell on his shoulders as the leader of the task force and the one heading up this plan.

His gut churned with both fear and anger.

Harlow should have moved closer to him, and he should have been right next to her, protecting her, before he'd called it off for the day, before the others had moved from their positions in the woods...

He could go over everything that had gone wrong later. Right now, he had to zero in on one thing.

Finding Harlow.

God...please...please keep her safe. Help me find her.

Desperation gripped him.

The sky remained a dim gray, but darkness had settled into the woods. He hated the prospect of turning on his flashlight and warning the man who'd taken Harlow. He'd much prefer to sneak up on him, but he didn't have night-vision goggles. His flashlight in his hand, he wanted to shine it and catch a glimpse of something, someone, or a trail. Signs of the man dragging Harlow.

His heart beat faster.

The killer had perfected his abduction techniques; he knew how to disappear in these woods.

He slid his finger to press the button but suddenly heard a voice. He resisted turning on the flashlight and stopped.

Nell whined.

He crouched next to her and petted her. "Quiet, girl."

Nell obeyed. She was such a smart dog.

And Wes listened.

"Stop? What are you doing? Where are you taking me?"

Harlow! A measure of relief surged—at least she was alive, and Nell wouldn't be used to search for a cadaver. An engine rumbled to life. They were running out of time, but the engine noise allowed him to communicate with his team.

He spoke in low tones so his backup would hear. "She's in the woods, close enough for me to hear her. Start closing in but don't scare him off again. Protect Harlow at all costs."

Stepping slowly, carefully, toward the direction of the voices and the vehicle preparing to leave—giving the killer a chance to escape with Harlow—Wes whispered so low he wasn't sure anyone had received the message over their mics because he got no response.

He heard grunts and more sounds.

A vehicle door shutting.

No! He couldn't lose her. If the killer drove out of here on the forest road, they might not find her before it was too late. They might never find her.

He released Nell's leash, then raced through the woods.

God, please let me get there in time.

Please help me save her. Please keep her safe.

He repeated his pleas in his heart as he ran, his gaze laser-focused in the waning light to hop over fallen logs, avoid rocks and boulders. Sticks and bushes.

If he tripped, she could die.

He stumbled into an area covered in pine needles—*Thank You, God*—then sprinted into an opening.

An old gray van was parked on the forest road. Holding his gun at the ready, Wes stepped slowly around to the far side. The driver's-side door was open. A man ran around the front of the van and was heading for that open door.

Wes raced to prevent him from getting in, aiming his gun at the man he now recognized as Martin Barnes.

Barnes also pulled out a weapon and aimed it at Wes.

"Let her go, Barnes!"

Barnes fired.

Wes fired.

At the same time. Wes dove for cover behind the van, a bullet grazing his shoulder. "Give it up, Barnes. It's over. You try to get into that van, and I'll shoot you before you can. There's nowhere to run. Nowhere to hide. We know who you are now."

The ground pounded; someone fleeing.

Wes peered around the van, shone his flashlight and saw the man disappearing into the woods, and shouted over his mic. "Suspected serial killer Martin Barnes is escaping! I need backup."

Not again...

He should have hit Barnes, but the man had ducked as he'd fired his weapon.

Wes raced through the woods at full throttle, chasing after the killer. At least they had a face and a name, and Martin Barnes wouldn't be able to hide in plain sight. They knew that Martin had been the man to abduct Harlow, and they would confirm he was the serial killer too. The manhunt was on. He couldn't escape the law enforcement along with the community closing the net in on him now.

Wes was forced to stop to drag in a much-needed breath and accept the sinking feeling that he'd lost Barnes. He shone the flashlight around, caught his breath and kept moving. But finally stopped.

He'd lost Barnes.

Again.

Fail, fail, fail… The mission had been a fail or would be a complete fail if they hadn't learned the killer's identity.

But the cost had been high!

Harlow…his heart nearly stopped at the thought of her. *God, please let her be okay.*

He raced back to the van to find Nell sitting at the back doors.

Alerting?

Signaling…a body? He almost dropped to his knees—

"Help!" Harlow shouted. "Get me out of here!"

"I'm coming. I'm here!" He grabbed the handle on the double doors. They were locked. He ran around to the vehicle to search for the keys and found them in the ignition. That made sense—the van was still running. He turned it off and his heart seized at the realization of just how close he'd come to losing Harlow. If the killer had driven off with her, they might never have found her...or before it was too late.

And she'd trusted them.

Trusted *him*.

Would he see that same trust in her eyes that he'd witnessed before? Or had it diminished or fled altogether? Anguish coursed through him. He pulled the keys from the ignition, then rushed to the back of the van. His hands shook as he tried to stick the key into the lock. Nell barked and underbrush rustled, twigs snapping as fellow task force members on this sting operation came running to his aide.

"Barnes is in the woods," he said. "He got away."

"Barnes? Martin Barnes?" the sheriff asked. "You're sure?"

"Yes! Keep searching for him. Helicopters. Dogs. Whatever it takes. I need two people to stay here at the van with me to protect Harlow." Wes flung the doors open.

Harlow sat on the floor, a black cloth bag over her head. Her wrists and ankles were tied.

The site nearly undid him.

"Harlow!" He scrambled into the van and dropped to his knees next to her.

Wes tugged the bag off her head. He set his flashlight to stand on its own, and in the dim light of the van, took in her fear-filled eyes and watched the relief surge in a flood of emotion. His heart pounded— all he could think was to free her and take her into his arms.

Forever.

Forever keep her safe.

He dug a pocketknife out and cut the ties on her wrists and then her ankles. Finally free, Harlow flung her arms around him and pressed her face into his shoulder. He wrapped her in his embrace and held her close enough to feel her body shuddering against him. Shutting his eyes, he silently thanked the Lord that she'd survived the terrifying ordeal.

He never should have put her in this position.

Comforting her, he said, "Shh, honey, it's okay. You're safe now."

I'm so, so sorry. We never should have taken the risk.

This disaster was all on him.

I could have lost you tonight.

He would send her back to Denver tomorrow with a 24/7 protection detail in place until they caught Barnes.

Never again. Never again would he risk her life.

FIFTEEN

Harlow tried to hold back the tears of relief, but they came out in dry sobs against Wes's shoulder. She held on to him for dear life, some inner fear lurking inside that Martin would tear her away from him again, as the adrenaline shuddered out of her. Seconds turned into minutes until she wasn't sure how long she'd been in his arms. Once the fear subsided and the relief that the danger was well over settled in her heart, she knew she should let go of Wes. But in his embrace, she felt safe and protected in a way she hadn't realized she needed. Or…wanted. And Wes's strong arms, his sturdy chest and soothing words filled that need in her. She'd just been thinking about being in his arms moments before Martin had darted Nell and taken her away.

Wes…

Why did it have to be Wes who'd come for her? Or Wes, the only man who *could* comfort her, or that she *wanted* to be here? She didn't want to leave his arms, but neither could she stay in them so long. She slowly shrugged free, discovering that he seemed equally reluctant to release her.

He lifted her chin, forcing her to look into his dark gray eyes. The pain she saw there knifed through her.

"I'm sorry this happened, Harlow." His voice cracked. "Are you okay? Did he hurt you?"

She shook her head and rubbed her arms, the chill of the night—or maybe this terrifying van she'd been stashed in—getting to her. "I'm fine."

He gripped her arms. "This isn't on you, so don't blame yourself."

She could tell he held back anger, but it

wasn't directed at her. They would debrief and go over what had gone wrong.

"We were all there and saw it happen. There was nothing you could have done, so I don't want you for one minute to blame yourself. Instead, let's be grateful that you're safe now, and that we know who is behind the abductions and likely the serial killings. Martin Barnes will pay."

Soaking his words in, she hoped she could take them to heart. "I'm cold. Can we please get out of this creepy van?"

He hopped out first, then helped her get out. She didn't need his help. Not really. But then again, her legs were shaky, so maybe she did. She knelt to hug Nell to her and listened to the others as they talked about what was happening.

"Evidence techs are on the way. We'll process the scene first, then haul the van out and impound it for evidence." The sheriff's voice droned on, but Harlow tuned him out while she let Nell lick her face.

She needed to take a few moments to

compose her emotions. Someone placed a warm jacket over her shoulders. She accepted the offer, stood and turned to see that it had been Wes. She could have guessed, but she hadn't expected the tenderness in his eyes.

A deputy and a ranger returned to the van, both out of breath. "No sign of him out there."

"He won't get far. We've put alerts out to all law enforcement entities."

"Please take her statement now, sheriff," Wes said. "I want to get her out of here."

Wes stepped away and the sheriff moved into her space. She shared all the details she could with the man and knew she would be repeating it all when the task force met again. Martin Barnes could be connected to two of the women, Cassidy Leidel in Yellowstone and Valentina Silva in Utah. He was the man who'd tried to abduct Harlow the first time, and he fit the profile of a serial killer. Even though they believed they knew who the killer was now, any detail she'd learned could still help them to locate him or could serve as additional evidence to convict him later. Every detail counted.

When she was done, she turned, took a step, and her legs almost gave out, but Wes was there to steady her. He maneuvered her away from the van and over to an SUV. His SUV. Someone had brought it to him on the forest road. He also held Nell by the leash for her but handed her dog off.

He had thought of everything. Another vehicle pulled up, before she could get into the SUV, to add to all the other law enforcement vehicles. Out jumped Chris Fuller—her fellow RMKU officer—along with his spaniel, Teddy. From around the other side of the vehicle came her colleague Lucas Hudson and his border collie, Angel.

Startled to see them, she huffed an incredulous laugh. "What—what are you doing here?"

Though Chris grinned as if he was glad to see her, his expression remained serious behind the grin. "Tyson got word of the operation that was going down." He glanced over her shoulder.

Nodding to Wes behind her?

And Lucas smiled, too, though, again— the smile was tenuous. Worry poured from his eyes. "Looks like we got here in the nick of time."

Wes had obviously gotten the go-ahead from his boss, Special Agent in Charge Michael Bridges, who must have, in turn, spoken with Tyson.

"But that doesn't explain why Tyson sent you." Alarm rolled through her. Tyson didn't think she could do her job without their help?

"We got wind of it, too, okay?" Lucas said. "Chris and I decided to catch a flight early this morning. We just got to Yellowstone a couple of hours ago, but it took a while to make our way here, and then we had to wait. But we're here for you, Harlow."

Her heart warmed at the sight of them.

Chris rubbed Teddy behind the ears. "Now that he's out there, trackers are needed, and we're here to offer our services...and to see that you're okay."

He took another step forward and hugged her, apparently not concerned that the action wouldn't appear professional. She savored his friendship and the warmth of his arms around her, and that of Lucas as well, then knelt to pet their K-9s. She really missed the training times they had in Denver. Harlow remained kneeling and loving on the dogs, including Nell, while Wes filled her RMKU officers in on what had happened so far and where they could help.

Angel was a SAR—search and rescue—dog and could be used to search for the killer, not just for someone who had gotten lost and needed rescuing, while Teddy was a tracker. The dogs could be used to find Martin, though they each had different skills.

Harlow ran her hands through Nell's fur. "And you found me, girl, didn't you?"

"The faster we get out there and find him, the better." Special Agent Ricky Shore had joined them. "We'll search for a couple of hours while the moon affords enough light. Your dogs should be able to help you avoid any hydrothermal activity."

"Teddy can track better at night, and we're adept at working night. I'm assuming time is of the essence if we're going to stop this killer."

"You assumed correctly."

"Probability of detection is far higher at night." Lucas looked at his RMKU counterpart, Chris, and nodded. "Let's get to it."

They pulled their dogs away, and Harlow slowly stood. She turned and, of course, Wes was right there. She wanted him closer.

Her heart warmed that her friends had

come to help because they were worried about her. "I feel like we need to be doing something. Like I need to help. Nell could help too. She could maybe detect the scent of death on him, because we suspect he's the killer. In fact, I think that's why she started barking back at the pool."

He gently gripped her arms and leaned closer. His voice was low and husky when he spoke. "I'm taking you back. You've been through a trauma, and I'm worried about you."

"Don't you need to debrief or regroup?"

"Yes. All in good time. Right now, the search is on for a killer. You were almost a victim. I don't... I don't know what—"

"You blame yourself, don't you? It was my idea. I'm not sure how things went so wrong, but we almost got him earlier, and we have to believe we'll take him down tonight."

But as Wes helped her put Nell in the back of his SUV, then ushered her to the passenger-side door, she felt the woods closing in around her. Felt the rough, sweaty hands of the killer manhandling her through those dark woods to his creepy death van. She couldn't shake the sense that this nightmare was far from over.

Wes drove back to the cabin where they'd stayed last night, the drive taking them half an hour. Harlow had remained solemn and quiet, and he was afraid to speak. He needed to sort through his thoughts and find the right words before he told her what he planned.

Wes was relieved when Ranger Kelly's vehicle pulled in right behind his SUV as they parked at the cabin, even though he should feel confident that Harlow was safe now that Barnes was on the run and being chased and caught, even now. Wes hoped and prayed.

Soon, very soon, Barnes, the rein of your terror will be over.

Every law enforcement agency in and around the park, the state of Wyoming and surrounding states, for that matter, were on the lookout for Martin Barnes. But Wes wouldn't drop his guard until the guy was in handcuffs, and maybe not until he was incarcerated for good.

"I don't think he's anywhere near here, but I'm not dropping my guard yet. So let's clear the cabin." She'd nearly been killed tonight, so he wanted to ask her to wait in the truck and to protect her, but he knew that letting her focus on her job would go a long way to help her move forward.

Harlow nodded, and together they made sure the place was safe.

Tonight had been much too close for comfort and he might never get over the terror that had gripped him upon witnessing Barnes take her, put a knife to her ribs and disappear in the woods.

That image played over and over in his mind and heart. Harlow would need counseling. And Wes was right there with her, in need of serious counseling, after almost losing a fellow task force member— Harlow—to a serial killer. He drew in a breath and then another and slowed his increasing pulse.

She wasn't going to like the news— that he was sending her back to Denver first thing in the morning with Lucas and Chris, the real reason they'd come to the park. Though their K-9s could be used to help in the search, he'd take that help as well. Still, once they got Barnes tonight, Harlow's and Nell's skills were no longer needed. Plus, they knew the killer's identity now and he wouldn't escape.

She was going back tomorrow, whatever came of the night.

The cabin cleared, he assisted her with Nell and spoke with Kelly, who was expecting help in guarding the cabin tonight. Kelly understood they should remain fully prepared for anything even though they both believed Barnes was on the run and had likely already fled the park or been captured.

God, please let us get him tonight.

Once Nell and Harlow were inside, Wes locked the door behind them and checked all the windows. The cabin was small. If he wasn't the head of the task force, he would whisk her away tonight himself. Whisk her away to safety.

After he'd put her in danger.

"Have a seat. No. Wait. Why don't you lie down and get some rest?" He gestured to her room. Was it only this morning he'd knocked on the door eager to share that he'd decided to take her up on her plan? The thought soured in his gut; anguish would keep him miserable for the foreseeable future.

"You don't have to treat me like I'm incapable, you know. I'm a police officer."

"And police officers are only human, Harlow." He rushed to her and gently gripped her arms, feeling the strength in her muscles and the softness there as well. "You're a very capable officer who was abducted and almost killed tonight." He softened his voice, leaned in closer, letting her know his next words were more…personal. He didn't care about the line she'd drawn earlier. "So forgive me if I'm a little overprotective. I'm here with you now. I'll be right here, I promise. I'm not leaving."

He felt the draw of her heart, her spirit, her eyes—and yes, he couldn't deny that he was attracted to her—and leaned close but detoured away from her lips to kiss her forehead. "Right here."

Never letting you go again.

As those words settled in his heart, he wasn't sure what to make of the way he felt about her. The words weren't true, because he was sending her away in the morning whether or not they had accomplished their mission. He would send her away but let her know that she had in no way failed. She was a stellar officer, she and Nell both were. He would recommend commendations. Maybe it was more that he wasn't ready to let her go yet, physically or in his heart, but he would have to do just that eventually.

Or would he? Did he have to let her go?

She peered at him, studying him as if she had a thousand questions.

He had those same questions—about them. If he didn't let her go in his heart, where did they go from here?

Especially if she was in Denver. But not now. Not tonight.

When she ducked her head and leaned closer, he led her over to the sofa and sat with her. She leaned in and he wrapped his arms around her. What would the rest of the task force, and the RMKU, think about their cozy little cabin? This was highly inappropriate, and yet, even if this wasn't Harlow, he would do everything he could to comfort a fellow agent or officer. But Harlow was the one to be with him, to sit next to him willingly. He sensed she needed the strength and protection he offered, and maybe it had everything to do with their personal past, present and… future.

"I'm here for you," he whispered against the top of her head, her soft hair tickling his nose.

She lifted her head and pushed away slightly, then rubbed her eyes. "I think I *will* lie down, after all. Please tell me the moment he's caught. And wake me first thing if I'm not up in the morning, so that I can continue to be a working member of this team."

She pinned him with her blue-eyed gaze, studying him, searching him, really…

He pursed his lips. "Get some rest. We'll talk tomorrow."

On the table, his cell phone buzzed. Probably texts from others on the team. While he didn't want to leave her—he wanted to keep holding her—she would press him for answers he wasn't ready to give. Not tonight.

He stood and grabbed his cell to look at the text, then glanced up as she headed for the room with Nell. She peered over her shoulder before closing the door. "I'll leave this cracked, if that's okay."

"Yes. And I'll be right here if you need me."

So she was scared, after all. Who wouldn't

be? She'd been through a terrible trauma, and he blamed himself. He'd have enough time later to think through his mistakes. At least she was here, well and alive.

After reading the texts that they were still out there searching for Barnes, Wes eyed the room where Harlow had settled into sleep—trusting him to protect her.

After he'd failed her.

SIXTEEN

Harlow sat on the bed, then finally eased back against the pillow. "Come on, girl. Get up here with me. No sleeping on the floor or in your crate tonight. I need to feel your warm body."

Yeah, Wes was out there and at least one ranger was outside—supposedly more were coming—but she couldn't get the fear, the images, out of her mind. Last night she'd gone to bed hoping Wes would listen to reason and allow her to be used as bait to draw the killer into a trap.

It had worked...but not in the way they had planned.

If only she could forget the moment he'd gotten the best of her, poked a knife in her ribs. At the memory, she lifted her shirt and, sure enough, he'd nicked her. But she wouldn't worry about washing that off until the morning. Shivers crawled over her body, and she wrapped the quilt around her and Nell both.

Get a grip. It's over. You survived. Wes... he saved you.

Nell whined and curled next to her. She pulled the dog closer to snuggle against her beneath the quilt. She ran a finger through Nell's fur. "And you..." she whispered. "You helped him find me. I know you did. Thank you, Nell."

And thank You, Lord.

Somehow. Someway. She would get over this night. She would likely be required to see a therapist before she'd be cleared to work again.

Would Wes let her work tomorrow? She'd assumed that he would, and she'd even brought that up, hoping to get some sort of confirmation from him. But he'd redirected her. Had that been a deliberate avoidance on his part? She'd seen something in his eyes. Something to the contrary. She hadn't wanted to latch on to it and question him, after all, he'd been so kind and tender. She could use another dose of his kindness and tenderness.

And that kiss.

Stop it. Just stop it.

She and Wes were not a thing, and they could never be together. Their past had proved that, and this brief time spent working well together meant nothing in comparison to what they had learned with their history together. Add to that, Martin Barnes would be caught tonight, and she would head back to Denver sooner rather than later. She would say goodbye to Wes with his good looks—those intense gray eyes, that strong scruffy jaw and dark hair. His ropy, muscular arms beneath his jacket or button-down white shirt, depending on the day.

And he was out there right now protecting her.

Exhaustion pressed down on her and finally her tumultuous thoughts slipped into nightmarish dreams of her running from Martin Barnes, chasing him. He grabbed her and dragged her away into the thick, black darkness where he lived.

Sucking in a breath, she sat up and gasped, trying to calm the fears. The dreams. She couldn't believe she'd actually fallen asleep and was pretty sure she had screamed and woken herself up.

But if that was true, then where was Wes? She had no doubt that he would have rushed to check on her, especially if she'd been screaming. And if it wasn't true and she hadn't screamed, then what sound had woken her? She hated the fear that gripped her, almost paralyzing her. Her overactive imagination had to be working overtime. That was all.

Nell whined next to her and licked her face.

"It's okay. I'm okay, Nell."

Nell barked and jumped from the bed.

"Shh. You'll wake Wes up."

No. Wait. Wes had made it clear his mission in life—well, tonight anyway—was to protect her. She didn't blame him for what had happened, but could tell he blamed himself, and maybe he'd gone overboard in his tenderness. But if he was protecting her, then why hadn't he come into the room when she had screamed?

That was it. She had to find out. She threw the quilt off, quietly slid out of bed and crept to the door to peek out into the living area. In their time together, she was accustomed to seeing him sitting up, wide awake, in the middle of the night or pacing. She fully expected to find that was the case, so she was surprised she didn't find him doing either of those two things now.

Harlow quietly moved across the small living space and peaked into the room where he would have slept, if he ever slept.

The door was wide open—and no Wes.

Dread curdled in her stomach and her heart rate jumped from a gentle thud to a frantic pace. Moisture rushed to her hands.

"Wes?" she asked softly.

Please let him answer. Please let him answer.

But Wes didn't answer.

No way would he have left her here alone in the cabin. Unless…wait…he'd just stepped outside to talk on his cell so he wouldn't wake her. Or he was speaking with one of the rangers there to protect her. She rushed to the door and pressed her hand against the knob. But what if something else had happened to him? Going out there into those dark woods could be dangerous.

Ranger Kelly. He would know. Relief whooshed through her.

Wes had to be talking to him; that was all.

Hand on the doorknob, she sucked in a calming breath as her gaze slid around the room behind her and landed on Wes's gun.

On the floor.

Wes fought the darkness edging his vision and shook off the dizziness. He felt bruised, like he'd been haphazardly dragged. His eyes were open, but the space was dark. Cold and dank. Smelled old and dusty and like oil and gas. Like a workshop or a shed maybe. He waited for his eyes to adjust. Moonlight cut through a covered window providing enough dim lighting so he could get his bearings.

And Harlow.

Oh God, please save Harlow!

How had Wes landed in this shed, his hands tied in front of him and his ankles bound? He'd failed. He'd let everyone down, but especially Harlow.

He tried to break free of the ties; would continue to work on them until he was free. Him being here could only mean one thing: the killer was still out there.

Had they got it wrong and Martin Barnes wasn't the killer? No. It had to be him. The man hadn't fled the park and wasn't on the run like they'd all suspected. And this time, he'd taken Wes—gotten him out of the way because Barnes had decided that Wes needed to go. Wes was standing between Barnes and Harlow at every turn, every attempt to take her.

Once Barnes got Wes out of the way, then he could go back to his game the way he liked to play it, abduct Harlow in the woods. He seemed to get a thrill out of fighting and winning. Taking her out while she was sleeping wasn't any fun to a psychopath like Barnes. But now with Wes tied up here, he could try again to snatch Harlow, get his adrenaline rush from overpowering her, and be successful this time in his own eyes. That was the only explanation. Unless…unless he'd gotten Harlow already while she was sleeping. Wes couldn't know. There was no way for him to know.

God, help me!

But he did know one thing. Barnes wanted to kill the woman Wes loved. He had been too young and stupid, too hardheaded to admit just how much she'd meant to him back at the academy. He'd been all about himself and moving up in the FBI world, and when Harlow had walked away, after their ridiculous blow-out argument, he'd let her go. He should have been strong enough, man enough, to apologize to her and make things right.

If given the chance.

God, all I need is a chance. Please, please let her be okay. Please send someone to help her. To save her.

If given the chance, though, he could make things right now. Today. Even though he wasn't certain that Harlow would want another chance with him, he would take the risk. He wasn't that stupid guy from the academy.

He was a man in love.

A man on a mission.

An incredulous laugh escaped. Why did he think she needed his help? Harlow could save herself. Of course, with God's help. They both needed God's help right now. And maybe…maybe he needed her to save *him*, but that could be exactly what Barnes wanted.

Frustration boiled and Wes thrashed around as he tried to free himself.

Don't come for me, Harlow. Don't look for me—as though she could hear his silent pleas of the heart.

He squeezed his eyes shut and tried to push down the growing fear. He tried and failed again to break free of the ties. And if he were to get free, he could have a long way to go in the woods before he found civilization. That would do Harlow no good. Why hadn't he gotten her out of this park and out of the state of Wyoming, delivered her to Denver himself, instead of staying in the park one more night?

Idiot.

Why, oh why?

He could beat himself up later. He had to get out of here and save her. To call someone. What had happened to the ranger standing guard outside? Had the others ever joined him? Had Barnes killed him? Why kill the ranger and bring Wes here?

Wes was able to maneuver to his feet. All

he could do was hop, and if he escaped, he'd have to hop his way out. He hopped over to the door of the shed and tried to open it, but of course it was locked. He hadn't expected it to be unlocked, but he had to try. Using his shoulder, he shoved against it repeatedly until the pain was too much. He sat near the door and positioned himself to kick it open.

Pausing, he angled his head. What was that sound?

A vehicle idling outside. Someone coming to help? Or was it Barnes coming back to finish the job? He scrambled to his feet, getting dirt in his mouth with the effort. He hopped over into a dark corner to wait, while he visually searched the shed for a tool that he could use to defend himself, and maybe, just maybe, take this man out once and for all.

Wes spotted a shovel.

The same shovel used to bury his victims? Except, wait, this couldn't be Martin Barnes's shed—he didn't live in Wyo-

ming. What had he done with the owners?
He moved to the shovel and precariously
gripped the handle. He wedged the edge
against the ties on his ankles and worked
it back and forth. Back and forth.

There. Success!

The ties fell away. His feet were free.

Wes prepared himself for the inevitable
moment he would face off with the killer.
With his hands tied, Wes was at a distinct disadvantage this time, though he'd
been taken out at the cabin while holding his gun. Now he vaguely remembered—the man had darted him, just like
he'd darted Nell. Only, the knockout drug
had been stronger and kept Wes out of it
long enough that he could be secured and
brought to this shed.

What about Ranger Kelly? If he, too, had
been darted, Wes hoped the ranger had
woken up and was now calling for help
and protecting Harlow. Deep inside, Wes
knew that was asking too much. Barnes
would never leave a ranger, or rangers, at

the cabin, at least alive, to protect Harlow. Barnes had secured Wes here to dispose of later—all part of his game. The more Wes thought about it, the more convinced he was that Barnes really was hoping Harlow and Nell would find Wes, and step into his trap. He was a psychopath. A serial killer. Grabbing his victims in the woods was part of Barnes's MO, after all, and to Barnes, this all made some kind of twisted sense.

Anger fueled him and adrenaline rushed through his veins as he waited to face off with this monster—his only thought to make sure he overcame Barnes, got out of there alive and found Harlow.

He'd never found himself so completely helpless.

A sound at the door drew his attention. Someone was unlocking the door. Wes braced himself for a struggle.

The door opened and dim lighting poured in from a security bulb outside. A big man's silhouette filled the doorway. The man cursed then rushed inside. "No way he got out." He spun then eyed the shadows. The corners.

Wes's time was short. He needed to make the most of this opportunity.

When Barnes turned his back on Wes, he rushed him, shoved him to the ground. He wouldn't win in a fistfight, so he scrambled to his feet before Barnes could get to his, then dashed through the open door. He raced to the idling truck. He fumbled with the door but got it open and clumsily scrambled inside. With his tied hands, he reached to shift gears and drive away.

Hands gripped his shirt through the open truck door and yanked him out. He landed hard on the ground, the air whooshing out of him. Before he could even catch his breath, he turned in time to see the very shovel he'd used to free himself, raised high over Barnes's head.

Fury poured from the killer's dark eyes. "You're dead."

The shovel came down as Wes tried to roll out of the way. Everything went black.

SEVENTEEN

Harlow continued to follow Nell into the dark woods, running after her beagle. She'd given her dog a command. An awful command to search for the dead. Because what else could she do?

Still, Barnes could still have the scent of death on him that had triggered Nell earlier, and if Barnes had taken Wes—she had no doubt that he had—then Nell would find the man.

And she hoped she found Wes alive and well, rather than his dead body.

Please, God, no. She pushed that thought out of her mind. She wouldn't think of it or dwell on it, but instead pray and hope and search for the man she loved. Why had it taken these horrific circumstances for her to admit she loved him, that she didn't care about their differences of the past? They could make it work. True love wasn't perfect and could be messy. She and Wes could do this.

If she got the chance to tell him, she would.

Please, please, please... Her heart's cry continued pleading with God as she ran through the woods, struggling to keep up with Nell. She'd found Ranger Kelly on the ground next to his truck. At first, she'd thought him dead, but he was only wounded—a knife wound, and he'd put pressure on it to stop the bleeding. He'd called for help on his radio, but help was too far out. Kelly had informed her that the killer had dragged a limp Wes into the woods, but he didn't know why.

She'd already known that Wes had left against his will because he would never have left his gun on the floor. Ranger Kelly instructed her, warned her even, that she should stay with him. That it was too dangerous for her to go in search of Wes alone, who was probably already dead. The words had pained him to say—that much she could tell.

Kelly appeared to fully believe that Wes was gone from this world. But if he was dead, then why drag him into the woods? Then again, that's precisely what Martin Barnes had done with any number of women, some they might not even know about yet. He'd killed them and then taken them to some random grave in the woods.

Despite her best efforts, she feared that Nell was leading her to one such grave holding Wes.

She had no doubt that Barnes wanted Harlow to follow that trail. No doubt that it was all a trap for her. Just like the trap they had set for him. Was she being stupid to walk into it? Maybe she was. All she knew was that she couldn't let him have Wes. So she held on to hope that he wasn't dead, and he would live long enough, at least, for Harlow to find him and potentially trade herself for him.

The trees were dense and prevented much moonlight from guiding her path. Harlow's mind raced as she followed Nell, clearly tracking something.

She couldn't imagine why she hadn't at least heard a scuffle in the room or why Nell hadn't barked and woken her. Wes would have put up a fight. Something. The hope she firmly gripped—more like desperately gripped—was slipping away. She grappled with it as she tripped over a fallen pine tree.

And yanked Nell back.

What was she thinking, that she could do anything to help him? But...she had to try. If only she could get the image out of her head of Wes being dragged off...dead. The ranger assumed that Wes was dead.

Assumed.

It couldn't be real.

She scrambled to her feet and brushed off the pine needles and leaves.

"Okay, Nell," she whispered. "I'm counting on you to find this man who must have the scent of death on him. Find him…"

And they would find Wes.

She hated to think about that truth and wouldn't voice the words. Nell continued on. The tears Harlow had tried to hold back surged and spilled down her cheeks, leaving hot, salty trails. She didn't care.

Wes…please…just be alive when I find you.

Any other outcome was unacceptable. She couldn't stand to think otherwise. Her heart couldn't take it. She should have told Wes how she really felt about him. Only, she hadn't admitted it to herself. Why did she have to be facing the possibility of losing him forever before she could admit that she was still in love with him and had never stopped?

Even if she found him—her throat tightened—alive, was it too late for them?

Oh God, don't let it be too late. I—

Nell surged forward, in that way that

told Harlow she was on to something. She approached an outbuilding. Too big to be a shed and not really big enough to be called a workshop. All the lights were out at a nearby house too. Her cadaver dog raced forward and alerted at the building.

Oh...no...

That could only mean one thing.

Death. Someone was dead inside that building.

Harlow nearly fell to her knees. Her heart hammered painfully as her limbs went weak.

God, please, no...

But her K-9 was never wrong. Hadn't she wanted Nell to alert...but to find Martin Barnes? The shed was dark and quiet and there wasn't a vehicle around. Martin wasn't here.

But death was here, inside the shed.

Harlow wiped at her tears. She was a professional. She'd come to find Wes. To save him. At the very least, she had to remain vigilante. Had to stay cautious and aware of her surroundings. She pulled her gun out. Not *her* gun. Wes's gun. She'd tucked it at the back of her pants.

Harlow approached the door that had been secured with a padlock. Great. She glanced down at her dog.

"Are you sure?"

Nell whined.

It can't be true. Wes is not dead.

Maybe someone else was in the shed. She didn't want to find anyone dead. She had only come out to find Wes.

The only way she was going to look inside this building was to break that padlock. If she shot it out, she could attract too much attention. She could draw the killer back. Still, if Martin Barnes had wanted her to follow, and she was at the right place, he would be somewhere near. Securing the gun at the back of her pants again, she found a fallen branch and used it to hit the padlock repeatedly. The padlock didn't break, but the door came off one hinge. Close enough.

She used her body to push against the door until one side broke off—it had rotted out a long time ago apparently. Lot of good a padlock did on a rotten door. But wait... it looked like someone had been beating against the door, trying to escape.

Heart pounding, a thousand silent prayers going up, Harlow stepped inside the space. She breathed in the scent of oil, dirt and grime, then flipped on a light switch and took in the surroundings.

And there... Her gaze landed on a form. A body.

Gorge rose in her throat.

Wes's body. He lay on his side.

Oh...

Her knees shook. She couldn't breathe as she walked forward and rolled him over to see the gash on his head, and the purple bruise. Tears blurred her vision as she took in his handsome face.

"Oh, Wes... I...loved you," she whispered.

But wait. His chest rose and fell. "You're breathing!"

He was alive. "Wes! Wes, wake up! Wake up before he comes back. We have to get out of here."

She grabbed his shoulders, half laughing, half crying with joy, and shook him. "Wake up!"

He groaned and his lids fluttered, then he opened his eyes. "Har... Harlow..." The sound of his voice croaking out her name was the most beautiful sound she'd heard in her life.

"Yes, it's me. Here, let me get you out of these ties." It took a few tries, but she was able to release the clasp and get the ties off.

Groaning, he rubbed his wrists.

"Wes, are you able to stand? We need to get out of here."

"Maybe. I don't know. But you should go. He'll come back. How...how did you find me?"

Harlow glanced around the shed. "Nell

brought me here, but why did she alert on this shed if you're…you're not dead."

Nell growled behind her, and Harlow whirled to see Martin Barnes standing there, holding a shovel like he would kill them both.

It was too late to escape.

Wes tried to focus past the pounding in his head as the familiar voice filled his ears. He tried to get up, but his body wasn't cooperating.

Harlow had twisted around but remained on her knees. She slowly rose and fumbled with something at her back.

"Move out of my way," Barnes said. "I have to get rid of him so you'll come back to me."

"Look at me, Barnes," Harlow said. "I'm not Cara. So I'm not coming back to you. There is no us."

Harlow, what are you doing?

Wes didn't like her tactics, but he recognized them. If she played along, maybe she could survive this until help arrived. Yeah. Help. All the law enforcement combing this park and Barnes slipped through their hands. Anger spiked through him, and his vision cleared enough to see what Harlow had been doing.

She continued to talk to Barnes, but she'd pulled a gun out of the waistband at her back and held it...she held it out for Wes.

"Move out of my way so I can kill him. He's the only thing standing between us. The only thing that has kept me from getting to you. And you came for him, just like I'd hoped, but now he won't stand between us anymore. I thought I'd already killed him, but now I need to finish the job."

"Would you listen to yourself?" she asked. "You're not making sense. First, you say that you're getting rid of him so I'll come back to you. Now you're saying that you're trying to get to me. I might have blond hair and blue eyes, but my name is Harlow not Cara. Harlow Zane, and I'm a police officer. A K-9 handler. What about the others? Tell me about the other women. Did you think they were Cara too?"

Wes suddenly wondered what had happened to Nell. Had Barnes shut her out of the shed?

"Huh?" Barnes frowned. "The others?"

"Yes. Women who had blond hair and blue eyes. They looked like Cara, but they weren't her, were they? Did you take them?"

A sob broke through, then he growled. "Yes. They were out in the woods in the park. Alone. They wanted me to take them."

"They didn't want you to take them. Then what did you do with them?"

Wes didn't like Harlow questioning the man, but she was buying them time as he slowly inched closer to Harlow and reached for the gun. Their fingers brushed as she released it into his hand, trusting him to take Barnes out. Since Barnes already held the shovel over her, he could crush her with it before she could whip the gun around, but Wes could use the element of surprise to his advantage.

"I killed them and then gave them a proper burial."

"Where? Do you remember where?"

"What?" He blinked and shook his head. "I keep that information in my notebook. Stop asking me questions, Cara. It's time to go."

"I'm not Cara, and I'm not going anywhere with you."

Barnes raised the shovel, his intention clear—to come down on Harlow's head the same as he'd come down on Wes's with that shovel. But he hadn't killed Wes. Maybe he'd thought he had, but the guy was crazy.

Wes chambered a round and slid his finger into the trigger guard, aiming as best he could with blurred vision.

"If you're not Cara and you're not coming back to me, then I can just kill you now. I can kill you both."

And he started to swing the shovel.

Wes took the shot, and the shovel came down inches from Harlow as Barnes dropped to his knees and fell face-first into the dirt floor of the shed, dead. His eyes were lifeless.

Relief surged through Wes, and he gasped for breath.

He squeezed his eyes shut. *Is it over? Really over?*

Harlow released a vocal cry of relief, then turned around. She knelt to press her face near Wes, gripping his shirt collar. Her warm tears dropped onto his cheeks as she cried—tears of joy, he would assume. "You did it, Wes. You saved us."

"No…it was you, Harlow. You saved us. You and Nell."

"Oh Nell!" Harlow jumped up, left him there, then opened the door. Nell barked and ran inside to lick Wes. Then she raced around inside the space until she alerted again.

Harlow shared a look with Wes. "I wondered why she'd come here. I thought… that's why I thought you were dead."

"I thought I was dead, too, so that makes two of us." Wes pushed himself up and let Harlow help him to his feet to steady him. Dizziness swept over him and he pressed a hand against a beam. Harlow at his side, supporting him, Wes crept slowly over to where Nell sat.

Harlow remained by his side. Comforting him. Encouraging him. How had he survived all these years without her?

Harlow gasped. "Look…it's a…it's a ranger's uniform."

He could make out a tag, and grief washed through him. "It's Cassidy Leidel's uniform. Barnes stashed it here before he buried her."

"Nell didn't pick up the scent earlier because we hadn't ventured out into the woods, but maybe the scent had grown stronger, at least strong enough she could smell it from the cabin where we stayed. And that's how she found you. I wonder if Barnes deliberately put her stuff here to draw Nell and me."

"We'll share everything and let others figure this out. I don't care about the why or the how. I only care that you're safe."

And he was alive.

"Ranger Kelly told me that Barnes had dragged you in the woods. You were limp, and he thought you were dead. He survived his injury and called for backup."

Harlow grabbed her cell. "I'm just going to call and let them know where to find us so we can get you some help."

She made the call, providing details about their location. Emergency vehicles and authorities were already responding to Ranger Kelly's call for backup. But as for this location? Glad she knew because he didn't have a clue. She made another call to the sheriff and two others on the task force. It wouldn't take long for them to get here.

And as if on cue, sirens resounded in the night. Wes hung his head. Finally, help would arrive soon.

Harlow was his hero. He closed his eyes as dizziness swept over him, and she helped him sit again. He opened his eyes to look at her, though he saw two of her.

"Thank you, Harlow, for coming to find me. But you put yourself, your life, in danger. Things could have turned out much differently." For a moment, he'd thought they would both die. She would die because of him. Because of his failure, first, then because she'd come for him. "Why... why did you search for me when you knew he was only going to kill you?"

"I know that you would do the same for me, Wes. I couldn't live with myself if something happened to you because of me."

He took in her sweet expression, and what he thought might be love pouring from her gaze, but then again, he'd been hit on the head pretty hard.

"Well, it's over now." Wes had shot Barnes center mass and seen the lifeless eyes, but he hadn't drawn Harlow's attention to that. "He's dead, and he can't hurt anyone else."

A siren blared right outside.

"We'd better let them know we're alive," she said.

"And Barnes is dead."

As he headed out of the shed with Harlow, Wes couldn't be more relieved about at least one aspect of this investigation.

But it meant that Harlow would be heading back to Denver and moving on to another assignment. They would go their separate ways. At the thought, a pang shot through his chest. His heart hurt more than his head.

EIGHTEEN

Palms sweating, Harlow walked into the hospital room where Wes had remained overnight so he could be monitored. Barnes had intended to kill him with the shovel to his head. He'd dragged Wes into the shed where he would let his body stay until he had time to bury him after he'd found Harlow or she'd taken the bait and showed up at the shed.

Wes rested in bed, his head bandaged, and his eyes closed—one swollen shut. Her breath hitched at the sight, and her heart stumbled. She'd seen him last night, of course, but seeing him all over again and now in a hospital bed, looking so helpless, nearly undid her. She slowly crept forward and tried to hold back the unshed tears.

She wasn't someone to cry a lot. Over the years, she'd had to work hard to prove herself strong and capable, especially in her role as a police officer. Now a K-9 cadaver dog handler. But the last few days had been so emotionally charged, that the tears came more often.

Chris and Lucas had agreed to watch Nell for her while she came to the hospital, and then they would all fly back to Denver together this afternoon.

They had caught her up on the latest news she'd missed since being in Wyoming. She was shocked to learn that Shiloh, the special K-9 training to work with the deaf, wasn't going to make the cut, after all. And poor Jodie Chen, the admin for the RMKU was devastated. All the news made Harlow realize how much she was looking forward to getting back to Denver to see her friends.

And…they shared that Wes had actually

been the one to inform Tyson and request two team members come out and escort her home. He'd known she would need their encouragement and support.

Wes…he'd gone out of his way to think of her needs, to put her first and protect her. She didn't for one minute blame him for the things that had gone wrong in their investigation. She would simply be grateful for what had gone right.

They had worked together and stopped a serial killer dead in his tracks.

Stubble grew on Wes's jaw, almost forming a full beard. He'd always had a smooth jaw in the past, and she wasn't accustomed to seeing him like this—scruffy and rugged. Still, he was handsome either way. He made her heart pound regardless.

She reached for his hand, pressed hers over his tanned skin, and swallowed the lump that sprang up in her throat.

"I wish you could hear me now," she whispered, "but I guess you're sleeping. I thought you weren't supposed to sleep."

But maybe they'd given him the go-ahead to get some rest after his head injury. "I... I'm going back to Denver this afternoon, Wes. I wish I could stay longer and see you fully recovered."

Wes suddenly opened his gray eyes, which had always been so intense, and right now they seemed to stare right through her. She couldn't move. Couldn't breathe.

A slight grin emerged, and he gripped her hand, showing himself stronger than she'd expected for someone lying in a hospital bed.

"Harlow..."

She returned his smile. "Wes."

"Back in the shed...when you found me. Do you remember?"

"Of course. I wish I could forget, honestly." Frowning, she huffed a laugh.

"Did you mean what you'd said?" He tugged her closer, surprising her.

"I'm not sure what you're talking about."

"I thought I was dreaming, but the words

pulled me out of the darkness. Tell me what you said was real and I didn't imagine it."

That knot emerged in her throat again and she couldn't speak. Should she? Once she said the words—again, with him conscious—there was no going back. "I said… I said that I love you."

There. It was out in the airwaves for him to hear.

He looked away. "When you thought I was dead. But I'm very much alive. Did you mean the words? Do you feel that way—" a tenuous smile broke his serious expression as he stared at her again "—when I'm alive?"

He hadn't said the words to her, but she could see the love in his intense gaze and no words were necessary. The tears she held back—tears of joy—broke free and streamed over her smile. "Yes."

With both arms, he gently pulled her forward until he could kiss her. "I was a fool to let you get away before. I hope you know I'm not that foolhardy stubborn man anymore."

"Even if you are, I don't care."

He kissed her thoroughly.

A nurse entered the room and cleared her throat, interrupting the moment. Harlow eased away but still held his hand, remaining connected so she could continue to float on this cloud. But a storm moved into her thoughts. "What about our jobs? You live in Wyoming and I'm in Denver right now. I also heard that you were offered a promotion to the Atlanta office."

He chuckled. "Oh, is that all. Well, Dad came in this morning, and we talked about Mom's improvement."

Harlow wasn't sure how this was connected, but he'd been hit in the head, after all, and she would go along with it. "Yeah? She's doing well?"

"Yes. Much better. Plus, Dad is going to retire, and he can be there for her, which means I don't have to be around so much or even in the same state."

Her pulse jumped. Was there hope? "What are you trying to say, Wes?"

He lifted her hand to his lips and kissed it. Warmth flooded her down to her toes.

"I won't put my career first and lose you again, Harlow. If you heard I'd been offered a promotion to Atlanta, it sounds like you didn't hear the best part." He smiled.

"Well, I'm waiting. What's the best part? Are you going to make me drag it out of you?"

"That my response to that was to request a transfer to the Denver office."

Her breath hitched. What? She struggled to comprehend his words. To breathe again.

Denver? She was in Denver.

And now, Wes would be in Denver?

Before she could respond, he pulled her close again. "I don't want to waste another minute without you in my life. I love you."

Harlow belonged in his arms. Joy exploded in her heart. "I love you too!"

He kissed her again as more throats cleared behind them and a dog barked.

Harlow laughed and pulled away to see Chris and Lucas in the room with them.

"Nell needed to be here for the moment, and we got permission."

She gasped. "You knew?" And glanced at Wes to see the grin on his face.

Nell wagged her tail and rushed to Harlow, who knelt to pet her beagle—the dog who'd found and saved the man Harlow loved.

*****

Don't miss Tyson Wilkes's story,
Explosive Revenge, and the rest of the
Rocky Mountain K-9 Unit series:

Detection Detail *by Terri Reed,*
April 2022

Ready to Protect *by Valerie Hansen,*
May 2022

Hiding in Montana *by Laura Scott,*
June 2022

Undercover Assignment *by Dana*
Mentink, July 2022

Defending from Danger *by Jodie Bailey,*
August 2022

Tracking a Killer *by Elizabeth Goddard,*
September 2022

Explosive Revenge *by Maggie K. Black,*
October 2022

Rescue Mission *by Lynette Eason,*
November 2022

Christmas K-9 Unit Heroes
by Lenora Worth and Katy Lee,
December 2022